JAXON

JAXON

C.E. JOHNSON

Cover design: Shanoff Designs
Editor: Sandra Dee, One Love Editing

CHAPTER ONE

HOLLY

CURVEBALLS. Life is full of them, and I've caught so many that my glove of experience is thoroughly broken in. But every once in a while, it's thrown at such a high rate of speed there is no catching the damn ball. Instead, it hits you square in the jaw and knocks you flat on your ass. I guess today was that day for me.

My breath fogs up the cool glass in my front door until I finally get my key in, turn the knob, and push my way inside. The metal clasp on my brown leather handbag clanks in the quiet house as I plop it onto the end table next to my couch. I shove the door closed with my back and slide down to the floor as I stare into the one-bedroom bungalow full of boxes. None of this was part of my five-year plan, but here I am.

People always compliment my cheery disposition when they come into my store. Attitudes are contagious. Good ones, bad ones, all of them have an impact on others. So, I make it a point to smile every single day and try not to put the negative out into the world. But it can be brutal to constantly pretend that my life is perfect. I have problems just like everyone else. It's not a fake representation of myself because I am that woman too. I just don't make my downfalls public knowledge. This world is harsh and heartbreaking. And if I can help someone escape that constant weight of terrible news and sadness, then that's what I want to do. So, I keep my plights to myself and give every person that enters my life a safe and positive space.

But I'm having a hard time finding my happy-go-lucky attitude with my brother, Arlo, suddenly abandoning me and the dream we've created over the last few months.

Just an hour ago, I was enjoying a beautiful day with my friends at Kalina and River's house when he called and hit me with what he said was exciting news. But exciting isn't exactly how I would describe it. My heart was crushing with every word as I prayed it was a sick joke. After all these years of stability, I really believed that Arlo's reckless habits were behind him.

I tried to end the call as quickly as I could so I wouldn't make a scene in front of everyone. But Jaxon, the six-foot, intuitive, and extremely hot friend of River, witnessed my reaction to Arlo telling me he's leaving Katoka Falls. I turned around, and there he was, just like the protective overseer I came to know when Kalina went missing a few months ago.

With his dark brown eyes searching mine, I did what I do best. I gave him my best fake smile and tried to pretend everything is okay. Then I hightailed it back to the porch by Kalina because the last thing I need is for him to be so close to me when my emotions are running high. I remember the way his arms felt around my body when he tried to console me when I was so worried about Kalina. I sank into his warm, protective shield like a lost puppy who needed a new home and didn't want to let go. But Jaxon is off-limits because he's the best friend of my best friend's husband. And Kalina mentioned in passing that Jaxon has no interest in relationships, and my heart is too fragile for another heartbreak.

Soon after I sat back down, I could tell Kalina was picking up on my energy. And she wasn't the only one. Jaxon didn't buy a word that came out of my mouth because his eyes darted to me constantly. In fact, it felt like everyone's eyes were cautiously flickering in my direction every minute I sat there. This circle of friends that Kalina has now have all been through hell recently, and the last thing River, Kalina, Jaxon, Cole, or Zayn need is to be worried about something else. Especially if that something else is me. So I left early. They all tried talking me into staying, but I just needed to get out of the spotlight I felt was on me. Sure, this is just a little family drama, but sometimes, a lady just needs to freak the hell out before she stands tall and takes care of business. I was hoping that the ride home would bring me a little clarity. That I could find the good in Arlo leaving.

Instead, the whole ride home, all I could think about was what a mistake I'd made. *What the hell have I done?* I have owned a boutique shop called Juneberry for about five years in the small tourist town of Katoka Falls. The only reason I even thought about leaving that place and buying my own building was because of Arlo. He convinced me that I was outgrowing my current shop and that together we could purchase our own place and expand. Arlo has a rock store full of gorgeous geodes, crystals, and jewelry. But it's the gem mining that has made his business so successful. It's also a big tourist pull, and if my store were in the same building as his and vice versa, we'd be increasing the amount of foot traffic and hopefully sales to both of our shops. I was a bit hesitant, but with a recent increase in my rent, Arlo's suggestion sounded better and better. With the help and guidance of Kalina's banker father, after a few hair-pulling months, I got approved to purchase the perfect place for Arlo and me to set up our businesses. And now, he's just backing out. I was never supposed to do this alone.

The clock that hangs on the kitchen wall to my right ticks as the sun lowers, casting an orange glow through the small kitchen window. I should be picking myself up off this floor and prepping for the conversation I'm going to have with Arlo tomorrow. But there will be plenty of time for me to pull up my big-girl panties and deal with the bullshit he's about to put me through. Right now, I deserve my moment to be sad, afraid, and royally pissed off.

There's only one thing to blame for all of this. Love. It makes people abandon all rational thinking and turn their entire life upside. I did that once, and it was the biggest mistake I ever made. I wish I could save Arlo from doing the same. He's fallen in love with some girl that I still haven't spent longer than five minutes with, and now he not only wants to abandon his successful business, he wants to move completely out of town with her. I can't think too much about how he's going to support his new plan of buying an RV and traveling the country because I have my own problem now. I have to find another renter for the other storefront in my building so I can afford this new gigantic commercial loan I have. I brush away a tear from my cheek and squeeze my eyes closed, knowing damn well I'm far more upset about my brother just giving up on all our plans so easily than I am about having to find another tenant. Even through all of Arlo's ups and downs, he's always been my best friend. And the fact that he chose to tell me over the phone that he's leaving me on my own in Katoka Falls makes me even more upset.

Two heavy knocks on the door against my back jolts my nervous system, and I let out a startled scream as my heart feels like it's jumped straight out of my chest.

"Holls? You okay?" Jaxon's concerned voice booms through the door.

With my heart still thumping wildly in my chest, I scoot to the side, reach up, and pull the door open. I must have been so lost in feeling sorry for myself that I didn't hear the rumble of his truck pull up. It isn't until my eyes float from his black boots up his long, dark denim jeans, over his black T-shirt that hugs every muscle on his cut chest, to his concerned eyes that I realize I'm still on the floor.

"What the hell?" he grunts, leaning down and putting his hands under my armpits. With little effort, he pulls me up and steadies me on my feet. "Why are you on the floor? Are you hurt?"

My hands rest on his bulging biceps as his grasp on me drops to my waist, holding firmly on my hips.

"No, I'm not hurt."

"Are you crying?" Jaxon swallows so hard I can see the bounce of his Adam's apple. His short, scruffy beard doesn't hide the muscles ticking hard on the back of his jaw. "Did someone hurt you? Who were you talking to earlier?"

My brain can hardly keep up with his rapid-fire questions. "What are you doing here?" I manage to form the words even though I melt a little more each second his strong hands grip my body.

"That look on your face at River's house...something is wrong. And I sure as hell don't like the way I just found you.

You don't belong on the floor, Holly. I understand some people like to handle shit in private. But if you want me to leave, you better convince me someone doesn't need to pay for putting those tearstains down your cheeks."

His fingertips grip a little tighter to me as his expression gains intensity. I don't know everything about his life, but it's enough to know that Jaxon doesn't hesitate to stick up for his friends by any means necessary. I witnessed that firsthand, but Kalina has filled me in on a few details about Jaxon, one of which is that he has sworn off serious relationships. And that's one of the reasons why I can't act on this strong attraction I have to him. The other is Kalina. She's not only my best friend, but we also work together at Juneberry. If something were to happen to make things weird, I don't want Kalina to be in an awkward position. And all of that means I need to keep the drool in my mouth and my hands to myself.

"No, no one needs to *pay*." I drop my hands before I lose the ability to take them off of him. "I'm just throwing myself a small pity party, but I'll be fine."

I curse under my breath as Jaxon slowly drags his fingers over my hips until I lose the warmth of his grip completely. He clears his throat and takes a step back.

"Pity party about what exactly?"

"I'm just having a hard day." I force a smile, but his expression doesn't falter in the slightest, and not one muscle in Jaxon's body is at ease. "It's not a big deal, and no one hurt me. I'm just being selfish."

"Every once in a while, it's okay to be selfish. Do you still have my number?" he asks.

"I'm not sure. I'd have to look. Why?" Jaxon wrote his number down for me on a piece of Juneberry stationery when Kalina was missing. But when all that dust settled, I got rid of

Jaxon Judge's phone number so I wouldn't be tempted to use it.

He puts his hand out. "Can I have a piece of paper and a pen? Or better yet, just give me your phone. I'll program it in."

Oh shit. Oh shit. I can feel the stunned look on my own face as he stands stoic as ever. "Wh...um...why?"

Instead of answering, he just bounces his hand and tilts his head, giving me a killer smirk that I'm sure has just caused some sort of seismic activity in the earth beneath my feet because my knees are shaking. It takes a hell of a lot more than a half smile to heat up my underbritches, but that's why Jaxon is so dangerous. I already know he's so much more than a sexy smolder and an embrace that feels like it could save me from the world exploding. He's loyal, smart, respectful, generous...the list goes on and on. I'm sure he's got his faults just like every other human on the planet, but much to my despair, I haven't seen them yet. With no excuse in sight, I have no other choice but to reach into my pocket, pull out my phone, and place it in his hand. He holds it up to my face until the click of the screen unlocking sounds. Before I can process how fast his fingertips fly across my screen, he hands it back to me.

"Listen to me. I get being the type of person who wants to put on a brave face and act like shit doesn't bother them. But you're human, and nobody can be that cheerful all the time. Something happened today, and for whatever reason you have, you don't want to talk about it. I respect that. But, if there's someone messing with you, I assure you, they won't be for long."

His protective nature does nothing for my self-control. No matter how strong a woman is, it always feels good when someone looks out for you. Knowing River and his friends have ways of finding things out, and before this gets out of hand, I know I just need to tell him.

"It's nothing like that. My brother is leaving town with his new girlfriend. We had plans. He was supposed to be by my side, both figuratively and literally, with the new building, and he's just up and decided he doesn't want to do that anymore. He was the last of my family left in Katoka Falls, and with him gone, I'm going to be all alone, and honestly, that scares the shit out of me. I should be happy for him, but all I can think about is myself. Which makes me feel selfish and dramatic."

Jaxon reaches for me, reclaiming the space he put between us. His tight body has turned soft, and that calming embrace that I remember envelops me again. I nuzzle into him for a moment, feeding off the safety and his faint scent of leather. "That's not being dramatic, Holls. And you're the least selfish person I know. You have every right to be sad. I'm sorry you have to go through this. If there's anything I can do, just ask and I'm there."

I lift my head slowly and watch his eyes drift down to my lips. For a moment, I lose reality and press my body further into his. His hand trails down the center of my back, resting just above the curve of my ass. He moves in, and I panic, jumping back a few steps, losing every degree of the heat between us.

I tuck my hair behind my ear, wrap my arms around myself, and attempt to brush off whatever just almost happened. "In case no one has told you lately, you're a really good friend, Jaxon."

Jaxon's eyes narrow slightly as he runs a hand through his dark brown hair. "So they say. I'll let you get on with your night, but do me a favor."

"What's that?"

"Don't cry anymore. You're going to be all right."

"Thank you," I say softly.

"For the record, Holls...you aren't here all alone. And if you ever feel like you are, use my number." He taps the doorknob as he steps outside. "Lock this again."

I nod, and he gives me a wink that sends my insides summersaulting before I shut the door and lock it. A second later, I hear the roar of his truck engine as he drives away.

Every time I see Jaxon, the fire between us reignites bigger, brighter, and hotter than the time before. But never have I been so close to kissing him. And even though I wanted to press my lips onto his, tell him to take me to bed, and live out the scenes that have plagued my daydreams for so long, it could ruin everything. Which means that's the last time I get that close to Jaxon Judge again.

CHAPTER TWO

JAXON

I STARE at my name on the tall sign that stands just outside of my vinyl shop. Every time I look at it, I think of my mom. She's the only person that ever called me JJ. Since I opened this shop with some of the money Mom and Dad left me after they died, it felt only fitting to name it JJ's Graphics.

The chime in the front office rings out as I push the door open and walk inside.

"It's about time you got here. Good grief, Jaxon, half the day is over already," Steph says, grabbing a folder from the filing cabinet and rushing back to her desk.

I double-check my watch, making sure I didn't mistake the time before leaving the house. "It's...eight thirty in the morning."

"Exactly. I've already been here for an hour working on that design for the Sage Bear Brewery. After all, someone has to run this place."

My little sister is one of the strongest women I know. She got that from our mother. Her heart is the size of an entire country, but it runs on tough love and the occasional smack across the head. She's stubborn, driven, and independent as hell. I love that about her. But sometimes, it can get her into trouble because she has no problems telling anyone to fuck off.

"You're the one who wanted to have a hand in this business. Why you choose to come in so early on top of that is all on you. It's not like you need the money," I joke.

When our parents died after a drunk driver hit their car, we both inherited the massive fortune that has been with our family for generations. Some call it "old money," but I tend to refer to it as the curse. It's the curse that made my grandpa a heartless father and mine an absent one. My father was far from heartless though. It's one of the reasons he moved us to a small town in Georgia. He never wanted to raise us in the same money-hungry world he was brought up in. We always had an overabundance of money, but Mom was unwavering in the fact that we lived like we didn't. She was ever the philanthropist who would have given everything down to her last dime to charity. They made sure my sister and I got more than we would ever need, and the rest of their personal fortune was split amongst some of her favorite organizations. Their will included a letter where Dad told us he fully supported our complete disassociation from the Judge family media empire. He felt forced by his own father to keep the few remaining family members in the company, but he didn't want that for us. After that letter, Steph and I both sold our remaining shares in the company, and we never looked back. The separation from it all made us even richer, but no amount of money could repair the shattered hearts we got from losing them. They were amazing parents.

"Because I like it here better than sitting at home by myself." she says, laughing. "How was Kalina and River's party?"

"Fine." I sit down at my desk next to hers behind the tall customer counter and log in.

"That's it? No details? No complaining about Cole's competitive nature? No laughing at Zayn having fifteen pairs of socks in his truck in case his shoes get wet? Nothing?"

I shrug. "Cole was gloating as usual. But other than that, we just hung out. It was good."

She gives me a side-eye, and I can see it in her face that she thinks there's more to talk about, but instead of pushing me, she moves on. "Speaking of Zayn, he called me this morning. He's got a new logo, and he wants to get his new trailer wrapped. He should be coming in anytime now."

Her phone rings, and from my chair, I can see an identifying picture of her ex-boyfriend pop up with his name on her phone screen.

"Oh God," she groans as she reaches for the phone. "Levi better not be sick again. I'll be back."

Steph takes her phone call outside, and even though I try not to overstep, I watch her through the window as I struggle to control my heart rate. Just the mention of my nephew's name brings on a wave of dread that settles deep in my chest making it hard to breathe. I've hidden my anxiety disorder from most of the people in my life. Even the ones I'm the closest to. Although my sister knows I have a slight issue with anxiety, she doesn't know how deep it goes. And I intend to keep it that way. So, I watch those I love like a hawk and suffer in silence.

The door opens and she walks back into the office.

"Levi fell at school," she says, pulling out her desk chair and sitting down.

Like a semitruck has just parked on top of my chest, the pressure causes an ache in my chest. "Is he okay? Should I go get him? Maybe he needs to see a doctor."

"Jaxon, calm down." Steph puts her hand on my shoulder and looks me in the eyes. She knows that helps me but still lacks the knowledge that my brain is playing out every single horrific scenario possible. "He's fine."

"You're sure?"

"I'm sure. He just took a little fall at recess and skinned up his knee, but Tori made sure he was okay," she says, raising her eyebrows, and I give her the nod that lets her know I'm calming down. With that, she flings her chair back until she reaches her computer and scoots herself in. "I'm so grateful Tori works at Levi's school. It makes it so much easier to be away from him when I know there's someone I trust close by. I got lucky, didn't I?"

My sister was in a relationship for about a year with her boyfriend, Isaac, when she got pregnant with my nephew. I thought I was going to have to break his neck when they broke up shortly before she gave birth, but she assured me it was a mutual decision, and that Isaac didn't do anything to hurt her. It was a huge relief when that was proven to be true. Even though their relationship didn't work, they are still good friends. Isaac got married a few years later, and Steph and his wife, Tori, get along so well. I'm really proud of the way the three of them co-parent Levi.

"It's pretty awesome when everyone can be an adult, isn't it?"

"Which is more than I can say for the morons I've been going out on dates with lately." She rolls her eyes and sinks her hands into her brown hair and fluffing. I never notice a difference when she does this, but I made the mistake of telling her that once and got a Stephanie special, which is a nice firm smack across the back of the head. She pulls out a little mirror and puts on a layer of nude lip gloss, then grabs a small bottle out of her desk drawer and spritzes something on herself before I can stop her. Not even a full second passes before the scent of death invades my nose and my stomach turns.

"I told you," I say, fanning a paper to try to avoid any more of the stench entering my nostrils. "No perfume in the office. It makes me sneeze, dammit. It's literally my only fucking rule."

I try to make the most realistic sound of a sneeze I can as my desk chair smacks against the concrete block wall behind us, concealing my horrible effort.

"Jesus. I forgot not to do it when you're here. Chill."

Desperate to get away from it, I walk away from the desks. "I've got work to do in the shop anyway."

I stomp through the door that leads into the back shop where I work and rub my temples as I head to my bay in the back. My sister has worn her signature floral scent since my mom gave her the first bottle of it when she turned sixteen. But everything in my life took on a different meaning when my parents died. And that floral scent no longer reminds me of my awkward sister with braces going on her first date with a guy I wanted to break in half. Now it reminds me of the exact smell of the flowers at Mom and Dad's funeral. But I'll never tell her that. I refuse to take away the good memories she has with them. Even if it takes me to a place I'd much rather forget on a daily basis.

I lose myself in work until Steph shouts through the door, "Zayn's here."

I set my tools down and jog through the shop door and up to the counter in the office, where Zayn and Stephanie are.

"It's really good, Zayn," Steph says, walking past me back to her desk.

"What do you think?" Zayn asks as he pushes his new landscaping business logo design to me without even saying hello.

"I like it too, man. You did a really good job. And that guy on the lawn mower even kind of looks like you."

"I thought about adding some more trees over here." He points to a spot on the paper. "And maybe another flowering bush over here to add some color."

"Leave it the hell alone, Zayn. You're going to muddy it up. It's perfect and will look great on your trailer," Steph says from behind me, continuing to type away on her keyboard.

Steph grew up with my three best friends. They treat her just like their real sister, and no matter what she says, Stephanie loves those guys just as much. Zayn is the only one in our friend group of four that Steph rarely gives a hard time to. Cole, on the other hand…sheesh. The two of them fight like two rabid coyotes in the wild. But I pity whoever messes with one of them. They may fight with each other, but no one else is allowed to fight with them.

"Just take it before I find something else to add, then. I've got to be done with this anyway. We have a huge job coming up, and I still have guys on other projects who apparently don't know what a deadline is. When do you think you'll be able to have the trailer ready?"

"I can have it done tomorrow."

"Perfect," Zayn says, relieved. "Thanks, man. How much is it going to be?"

"Family discount," I tell him.

"Dammit, Jaxon. You're going to let me pay for this. Otherwise, I'll be forced to go somewhere else for all of my graphics needs. We've had this conversation before."

My friends know I have a hard time taking money from them. I don't need it, and there's a weird guilt I get from accepting it. It's a common argument River, Cole, Zayn, and I have whenever we're together. I always feel the desire to pay for everything because I can, and money doesn't mean anything to me. I'd rather use it to make other people happy, but I do understand that sometimes it can make them feel bad instead.

"Okay, okay," I say, holding up my hand. "Steph will get it invoiced tomorrow."

"Thank you. Oh, how was Holly when you checked on her? Is she okay?"

I hear the wheels under Steph's seat roll quietly on the concrete floor until she's next to me.

"She got some bad news and it kind of rocked her world a bit."

I glance down at Steph and see her over-the-top grin, and if she raises her curious eyebrows any further, they're going to end up in her hairline. I roll my eyes and try to ignore her.

"I'm glad it wasn't something serious. She's one of the happiest people I know, and seeing her upset like that was weird," Zayn says, tapping the counter. "That's not like her."

"No, it's not. She assured me she's fine but I'm keeping an eye on her just in case."

"I'm sure you are," he says with a grin. I shoot him a warning glare, and he takes note, but his grin doesn't fade. "Okay, trailer is parked outside. Let me know if you need anything."

"Sounds good, man." I watch Zayn walk out as I carefully

plot how I'm going to get out of this office without the third degree. I take one step before Steph rolls her chair in my way. "Steph, don't go there." I grab her chair and send her rolling at full speed across the floor.

She bolts up and runs in front of the door to the shop and plants her hands on either side of the door jam and her feet in the corners like a starfish.

"You do know I can move your entire body with one finger, right?" I ask.

"Don't care. So...Holly, is it? Wait... Isn't that River's wife's friend?"

"Yes, she is Kalina's friend, which is the only reason I made sure she was okay. Now, if you don't mind, I have work to..."

"Nu-uh. I know you stick up for your friends, Jaxon. But this seems...more than that. I think you like this girl." Stephanie's face lights up like a three-year-old who just opened up a dollhouse on Christmas morning.

"I can actually see the smoke coming out of your ears. You're thinking too hard about this. We're friends. That's it. Stop all..." I motion my hand around her face. "This. I told you before, relationships aren't my thing."

Steph's phone rings again, and she finally releases herself from the door to grab it from her desk. She shrieks and dances in place. "Fine. I'm busy with my own life anyway. Isaac has Levi tonight, and I just got a date," she says.

"Where did you find this one?" I ask, rolling my eyes.

"Levi's soccer practice."

"Great. So I won't have to travel fifteen hours to kill this one if he's stupid enough to hurt you." I prop the shop door open. "And don't forget, if you get in a situation..."

"Kick him in the nuts, poke his eyes with my fingernails,

and call you immediately." The boredom in her voice confirms that I've etched those words deep into her brain. Perfect.

"And if I don't answer on the first try?"

"Call Zayn. For crying out loud, do we have to go through this every single time? I'm an adult."

"Yes we do. And why don't we call Cole?"

She giggles. "Because one time he punched a guy before you got there, and you missed out on the fun."

"Exactly."

Stephanie starts laughing to the point of a loud snort coming from her nose. "That guy didn't even see it coming. He was too busy laughing at Cole's cat pajama pants I bought him. They should've been his first clue. A man wearing those pants in public doesn't give a shit about anything."

Between her contagious laugh and the image of Cole standing in that bar in those ridiculous pants with his cat's face all over them as he kicked the shit out of a guy who deserved it sends me into laughter too.

"I'll be careful," she says as the office phone rings.

I nod and head back to work.

———

THERE'S something about these kinds of nights that make the air in my house heavy. After working a full day, I came home to an empty house, ate dinner alone in front of the TV, and went to bed early. It's the same routine every night unless the guys want to hang out. We see each other in passing quite often but don't always get the chance to spend quality time together. We keep saying we're going to change that, but with all of us working, it's hard. Hell, we were barely away from each other when we were kids. Our bikes would be piled in my yard daily, and we'd be chowing down on pizza snacks and warm chocolate chip cookies Mom would make for us as we played baseball in the backyard or video games. You don't realize how awesome those days are until they are so far in your rearview mirror you can hardly recognize them.

Out of all of us, River has been the most adamant about not letting ourselves drift apart. Which is funny now that he's moved an hour away. I guess he's lucky that Zayn, Cole, and I don't mind that drive at all. Especially when we get to visit one of the best fishing spots in Georgia. We've already made a bunch of plans for the next few months, and I'm looking forward to the forced change of scenery.

I pull the blankets up to my chest and stare at the time on my phone. Almost quarter to twelve already. Stephanie knows she only has about fifteen more minutes to text me before I track her location and go hunting. She agreed to keep her phone location on if I promised I wouldn't get nosey until midnight. I could care less what she's doing, but I need to know she's safe. As the minutes tick by, the small muscles in my jaw ache as they twitch with worry. I set my phone down and run my hand over my short beard to stop myself from checking on her before the clock strikes twelve. My mind starts playing scenes of Stephanie lying in an alley somewhere when my phone chimes.

"Thank fuck," I mutter as I snatch the phone from my nightstand. Only once I look at the screen, it's not Stephanie's name that appears.

HOLLY: Just wanted to say thank you for checking in on me the other night.

HOLLY: Oh no! I just realized what time it is. I'm so sorry if it's too late.

I GET a third text at the same time as Holly's second.

STEPH: Everything is good. I'm home. Men suck. Love you, goodnight.

NOW THAT I know my sister is home and safe, my worry switches targets.

JAXON: It's not too late. Is everything okay?

EITHER HOLLY HAS BEEN at Juneberry for far too long today, getting it ready to open, or something is up.

HOLLY: Of course. I'm swell.
    JAXON: You're swell, huh? Not buying that. Spill it.
    HOLLY: I didn't text you to listen to my pity parties. LOL. I'm okay.
    JAXON: I like parties.

THAT'S A FUCKING LIE. I hate parties. Unless they only include my small group of close friends.

· · ·

HOLLY: Okay. I was supposed to meet Arlo, my brother, at the gazebo in town and he never showed up.

Never showed up are three words that usually trigger my suspicious instincts. But I don't know her brother that well.

JAXON: Maybe he was just late?

HOLLY: I sat in the park until after dark before he texted me that he wasn't going to make it but that we'll talk tomorrow before he leaves. I'm sad but I'm over it. I already put together an ad for the paper looking for a new renter for his side of the building.

The thought of Holly in that park on the side of town by herself in the dark makes my nostrils flare. I would have been a wreck just knowing she was sitting out there. How the fuck could he be okay with that and stand her up on top of it.

JAXON: I don't think you'll have a hard time finding someone to fill that space. Everything will be okay.

HOLLY: I guess I just needed to hear someone tell me that. Thank you.

Fuck. A swift smack to the chest wasn't what I expected to feel tonight.

.   .   .

JAXON: How is Juneberry coming along?

HOLLY: Some days it seems like I'll never get done and other days I feel ready. I'll be there from sun up to sun down until we open though. Which means gallons of coffee and pounds of take out. I'm optimistic I'll be able to get it all done with Kalina's help. Listen, it's late and I shouldn't be bothering you. Thanks for the nice words. They helped.

JAXON: You will never be a bother. Text every night if it helps, Holls. I'm here.

SHE SENDS a text with a big smile emoji, and I wait to see if those three little dots start to dance in the lower left corner anymore. When I'm sure the conversation is over, I plug in my phone, place it on my dresser next to me, and relax down into the pillows.

Because of my inherited wealth, I have no choice but to be very careful of the people I choose to let in. I made mistakes in the past that I refuse to ever make again. That includes getting too close. But I knew the moment my eyes touched Holly's light blue ones that she wasn't like anyone I'd known before. I can trust her, and that's why keeping my distance is so hard.

Falling for Holly could get messy real fast. So I have to focus on keeping our relationship platonic, my eyes to myself, and my hands in my pockets. Because touching her is like breathing the purest air. Holding her in my arms gives me the type of bliss I've never known. And the swell in my heart when her eyes lock on mine lets me know it would only take one tiny pin prick to make it burst into pieces. Now I just have to figure out how to keep Holly without taking it to a level that we can't come back from.

CHAPTER THREE

HOLLY

"I'VE GOT A PRESENT FOR YOU," Kalina says. A wide smile covers her face as she holds one of my favorite bars of soap in my direction.

"Gimme, gimme, gimme," I say, clapping my hands like a child. She hands it to me, and I take a long, slow sniff of the invigorating citrus aroma. "Thank you so much."

Kalina makes the best homemade soap I've ever smelled, and this margarita scent is one I try to hoard when she makes it in the summer. I ran out two months ago, and I've missed it in my morning showers.

"You're welcome. Thought you could use a little pick-me-up, and citrus oils are good for that."

"You didn't have to go through all that trouble for me. I could've waited until the summer for a refill. Though I'm not going to complain, of course." I smile and sniff it again. "I'm just stressed with the shop getting open and all this work we still have to do. But I know it's all going to turn out just fine. But thank you. I will cut this one into pieces and savor it."

"You don't have to do that. I made a whole batch."

Kalina opens one of the bins she hauled in from her Jeep and reveals an entire layer of the green-and-white soap with a perfectly placed soap lime on the top. She's been selling her soap in Juneberry for a few years now. It's one of my staple products, and hopefully, once this place is in order, she'll be able to make it right here in the shop instead of having to cart it all in every week.

"You're an angel."

I place the soap on the counter where the checkout will be and glance around the room. The boxes are slowly being emptied onto the tables and displays, but there's still a lot to be unpacked. With the taller ceilings, I was able to order a rustic, wood beaded chandelier to hang in the center of the store to match my boho vibe in the shop. But I'm still waiting for that to be delivered, as well as shipments from a few new small business vendors I've ordered products from. So we just keep unpacking, inventorying, and setting up the products as they come in.

Kalina puts her hands on her hips, looks over the big open space and through the large front picture windows that stretch from the ceiling to the floor. The building isn't old, but it isn't new either. It was built to look like a wood cabin, which fits the aesthetic of the entire town. The inside is filled with rich wood floors and creamy walls that I've adorned with a few pieces of artwork from local artists. I try to fill my shop with handmade treasures, a few racks of clothes from small designers, and lots of cozy vibes. When people walk into Juneberry, I want them to take a deep breath in and escape the world outside. That's my hope anyway, and I work hard to create that atmosphere for both my customers and myself.

"Okay. Before we get to work, let's get the elephant out of the room so I don't have to try to avoid the subject all day. What happened with your brother yesterday?" Kalina asks.

I push the stubborn curl that won't stay out of my face behind my ear and force the air back out through my lips. "He didn't show up."

"What?" Kalina shouts, dropping her hands and taking a step toward me.

"Yeah. He finally texted me after I had been sitting in the park for over an hour that he wasn't going to make it and that we'd meet up tonight before he left."

"That's unbelievable. Obviously, it doesn't seem like he's making good decisions here lately."

"We'll see what I get out of him tonight, but he isn't a teenager making mistakes anymore. He's an adult who fell in love and now he wants to give up everything for her. I can't stop him."

"No, you certainly can't. And you know I'm on your side always. But…"

"Please don't tell me something logical."

Kalina smiles. "Sometimes you have to do what makes you happy and not worry about how other people feel about it. That's what I had to do, and look at where it led me. I'm the happiest I've ever been in my entire life. So maybe try to see things from his perspective, and don't take him leaving as a personal attack on you."

"Dammit, Kalina. I told you don't be logical."

"I know. It's hard to watch someone you love do something that you think will be a mistake. But it might not be. You have to trust that they know what's best for them. Life is full of risks and sometimes taking them puts you on the exact path you're meant to be on."

"Oh, I know about that. Buying this place was a risk. Opening Juneberry in the first place was a risk. But how many people just give up their entire life and move away with someone they just met." Kalina slowly twists her pursed lips as she attempts to hide her giggle. It wasn't long ago Kalina and River took that exact route and ended up happy in the end. "I'm not talking about you two right now. You're the anomaly."

"I think it happens more than people want to admit, and just because it doesn't fit society's version of *normal*, then it's a terrible decision. River and I are proof that isn't always true."

I hate and love that Kalina can talk sense into me even in my most stubborn state. The perky, easygoing, happy Holly is the me I always want to be. But Arlo leaving so suddenly has shaken up my world, and for the first time in a long time, I don't know how to get that sunshiny feeling back again.

"It's just…" I say softly. "If Arlo leaves, I'll have no one. My parents are off riding gondolas in Venice or chugging beer out of a stein in Munich, or, hell, maybe even participating in the Running of the Bulls in Spain. They call every now and then, but with Arlo and I grown, they're off living their dreams. My aunts and uncles all live in other states, and my grandparents have been gone for a while now. I'll have no one."

Kalina grabs my hands with hers and faces me. "Okay. I'm giving you about two days to get this out of your system, and then I'm going to smack you." I start to laugh, and Kalina shakes my hands as she smiles. "You have me. Understand? I'm not going anywhere, and you know River loves the hell out of you. And with us comes three other large and intimidating men who would also do just about anything for you. You are so far from alone in Katoka Falls."

"I know," I say, squeezing her hands before we both let go. "You're right, and Jaxon said the same thing last night."

Kalina clears her throat and cups her ear, acting like she didn't hear me, and I cringe as I realize my mouth has just made an epic mistake.

"I'm sorry. You talked to Jaxon last night, did you?"

I grab a box from the counter, move around Kalina, and speed walk to the table in front of the window. Her fast footsteps keep up with me the entire way, but I pretend I never said his name.

"Just look at these stunning pillows Handcrafted Harvest sent," I say, pulling one out of the box and setting it up on display.

"Did he call you?" Kalina asks.

"This mustard color she uses in her designs makes everything else pop, doesn't it?"

"Holly. Fuck the pillows, I'm dying here. The tension between the two of you anytime you're together is enough to break a rubber band. Spill, spill, spill."

I laugh. "There's nothing to spill. He stopped by to make sure I was okay after I left your house the other day. I was upset, and he was very sweet. He ended up giving me his number and told me if I'm ever feeling lonely to call him."

She grabs the pillow I just set out and cuddles it against her chest as she leans over the table and puts her chin in her hands. "He stopped by your house that night?" Her voice cracks as her high-pitched tone echoes against the walls. "Wow. That's a first, as far as I know. So, are you two talking, then?" she asks.

"No," I practically shout and Kalina's smile only gets

bigger. "It's nothing like that. I just sent him a quick text last night thanking him for stopping by and being so nice."

I grab another pillow from the box and place it where the first one used to be. Kalina stands up with pure joy all over her face. "I like the blush you're wearing today."

"I don't have any makeup on."

"I know," she says, grinning wide and tossing the pillow at me. "It's called Jaxon."

"Why are you so excited about all of this? It wasn't that long ago you told me what Jaxon said to River."

"About the relationship thing?" Kalina asks.

"Yeah. That." I grab the now empty box and head back to the counter to grab another one. "River told you that Jaxon never wants to get married and hates relationships."

"He did say that. But things change. Kind of like how I said I never wanted kids."

I freeze in place as I stare at Kalina. "Are you...are you telling me something right now?"

"Oh gosh," she says, placing a hand over her chest. "No. But we've been talking about it. The point is, sometimes, things just change, Holly."

"And sometimes they don't. It would make things far too complicated for my liking. Anyway, we're just friends, and I have my hands full with this shop and my brother's drama."

"Well, if you ever want to go on a double date, just let me know."

"That's not going to happen," I shout as I head into the back storage room to destroy the boxes I emptied. All of that sounds just great until something happens between Jaxon and I. Suddenly Kalina is on my side and River is on Jaxon's side and I won't be responsible for that kind of complication in their relationship. I refuse to give the conversation any more attention even though my mind is filled with visions of Jaxon's hands on my body, his lips against my skin, and the way he would look on top of me.

It's nearly impossible to get Jaxon out of my head as Kalina and I work all day unpacking, moving, and organizing. We're both exhausted by dinnertime but I still practically have to throw Kalina out of the shop so she can go home and get some rest.

"Promise you'll call me later if you need a shoulder after talking to your brother?" Kalina asks with an empty soap tote in her hands.

"I promise. Thank you, and I love you, girl."

"You know I love you too. Bye." She waves as she walks out the door.

I break down two more boxes before grabbing my purse and locking up on my way out. The conversation with Arlo needs to be had, but I can't wait until it's over. So instead of going home first, I text Arlo that I'm heading to the park now. Hopefully, he actually shows up tonight.

ARLO'S SANDY-BLOND, wavy hair blows carelessly in the breeze as he rolls his eyes at me. How do you tell someone that they're making one of the biggest mistakes of their entire life and not have them tell you to fuck off? I don't know the answer to that question because that's exactly what Arlo just did. After a few minutes of silence between us to gather our patience, I can't help but feel that burning sensation in the back of my eyes.

"I'm worried about you."

"Well, stop it, Holly. Danica makes me happy and excited

to do something different with my life. I've been stuck in this town for years just for…"

My heart feels like an anchor that's just been thrown over the side of a boat into a bottomless pit. "For me," I say. "You've only been staying here for me, haven't you?"

He takes a deep breath and leans back against the wooden bench. "Holly…"

"It's okay. I should have known. You always have been the adventurous one. I shouldn't have pushed the new building on you."

"No, this is all my fault," Arlo says, lowering his head. "I should have spoken up when my heart wasn't in it as much as yours was. I just couldn't look you in the eye and break your heart like that. You were so excited, and I couldn't take that from you."

The guilt rages inside of me. "Like I've been doing to you this past week."

"Listen, I can't stand this horrible feeling, and I sure as hell can't leave tomorrow with things tumultuous between us."

"So you're saying if I keep being a bitch, you'll stay?" I say with a big grin but a tear rolling down my cheek.

"Awww, Junebug," Arlo says, calling me the nickname he's used for me since we were kids. He tosses his arm around my shoulders, pulling me into a side hug.

"I don't want you to go," I say, wiping the tears from my face as quickly as I can. I hate crying in public.

"I know. But you've got this. Trust me, you'll have no problem filling that ad in the paper. Someone will snatch that empty space up, and you can charge more than you were going to charge me. Just think, you'll be in an even better position when I'm gone."

This time, I don't even try to stop the tears as they cascade from my eyes and down my cheeks. Arlo does the only thing he knows to do when I start to cry. As if we were still fifteen and thirteen, he gently headlocks me and gives me noogies on the top of my head until I laugh.

He releases me and stands from the bench.

"Please, just be careful, and let me know where you are from time to time. Preferably more often than Mom and Dad let us know where they are," I beg as I stand, too, and wrap my arms around my brother.

His warm embrace envelops me as he kisses the top of my head. "You know I'll let you know wherever we end up after Colorado. I love you, Junebug." As our hold on each other loosens, I take a small step back, and he grabs hold of my arms and stares me in the eye. "I'll always be a phone call away. But we don't have to say goodbye just yet. Come to Duke's with us tonight. We're going to have a few drinks with Hubbard, Winsley, Danica, and a few friends as a send-off before we leave in the morning. I meant to invite you before, but you haven't been too happy with me, and I didn't think you'd be too thrilled with a going away party."

"I'd rather pluck my eyelashes out than have a few drinks with Hubbard and Winsley. Those two are always being menaces."

"Oh, come on. It will be a good opportunity for you to get to know Danica a little bit, and I really want you to come."

"Fine, I'll come. But I need to eat first. You and I both know it doesn't take much for me to get woozy."

"We'll be at Duke's in about an hour, but come whenever you're ready."

He pulls me in for one more quick hug, lets go, and speed walks to his car in the parking lot. My feet are still stuck in place as I look to the sky hoping it opens up and a rogue monsoon floods the roads, making them too dangerous to go out tonight. Am I being a child? Perhaps. Will I still be cordial to my brother's newly acquired partner in adventures away from Katoka Falls? Of course. Because I love my brother, and this is what he wants. Which means I am going to put on a happy face and accept what's happening. Even if I hate it.

I PULL up next to Arlo's car, hop out, and rub my stuffed belly. In hopes of having a few drinks without the awful whirly feeling of a buzz, I ate way too much, and now my cute fit-to-flare jeans make me feel like a stuffed sausage roll. My tight white tank is also not helping. Thankfully, I paired it with a floor-length kimono that I can wrap around myself. As I make my way around the corner of the building, there are cars lining the street in front of Duke's. Either there's a large influx of tourists I don't know about, or this is way more than just a few friends. I think about turning around and going back to my snuggly warm little house and watching reruns of old comedies. Instead, I open the door, and the loud country music blasts me in the face.

"Junebug!" Arlo yells, as he rushes across the room. He swings an arm around my shoulders and escorts me through the crowd of people up to the bar. Danica turns around, her short black hair swinging in and out of her face as she flashes me a fake bright white smile. It feels disingenuous, but I'm a little hard to please at the moment. I smile back and take the stool next to her and my stomach turns from her overpowering gardenia scent. Everything about her rubs me the wrong way but even if it kills me, I will have a relationship with this woman.

"Hi, Danica," I say, hanging my purse on the hook under the bar. "What are you drinking?" I point to her nearly empty glass, and her expression softens, which surprises me.

"I'm glad you came," she says. "It's Jack and Coke."

The bartender places a small square napkin in front of me. "I'll have a rum and Coke, and put her next one on my tab."

"Aww," Danica says in a new friendly tone, swinging her barstool toward me. "That's nice of you. Thanks."

"Of course. After all, it seems like you'll be a big part of my brother's life, which means you'll be in mine too. Do you have family in Colorado?"

Sometimes, there's nothing worse than small talk, but I'm desperate for it with Danica. I want to know everything I can about her. It seems my question about their first destination on their trail of adventure did the trick because not only has the bartender already brought us our drinks, but she's still talking, and I'm almost done with my first one. I guess I've opened a can of worms because she goes on and on about herself. As she rambles about a crocheted blanket she made in clothing class in high school, the bartender nods to my empty glass, and I nod desperately back. At this point, I'd love nothing more than to be a little woozy.

"Oh," Danica shouts over the music to the bartender. "We need tequila, please. Four shots."

My eyes feel like they're about to fall out of my head. "It's been a long time since I've done shots."

She moves in close, presses her face to mine, and before I even know what's happening, she holds up her phone and takes a selfie of us. Right as I'm about to excuse myself for a breather, I spot Arlo looking in our direction, and the happiness on his face is something I didn't realize had been missing for so long. In fact, I don't know if I've ever seen him so happy before. I turn to look at Danica who has also caught eyes with my brother, and she blushes. *Fuck. I'm a selfish bitch.*

She turns back to me, and her nose wrinkles as concern litters her face.

"Are you okay, Holly?"

Before I give her a generic answer, I take in what I've just witnessed. Truthfully, I am okay. More okay than I've been since that phone call at River and Kalina's house. "Yep. I'm totally good."

The bartender puts four shots in front of us with salt and limes. Danica hands me a shot and takes one of her own. I lick the back of my hand, pour a little salt on, then give it to her, and she does the same. Then she holds her shot glass up.

"To love," she says.

I clink my glass to hers and for the first time truly appreciate the love she has for my brother. "To love."

We lick the salt off our hands, shoot the tequila, and bite into the limes as both of our faces sour.

"Oh my God," she says, wiping her lip. "That is awful."

"It's the worst," I say, shoving the next shot in her direction.

We both laugh and do it again. And again.

"I hope you don't hate me for Arlo leaving." Danica's admission hits me hard. I did. I sure as hell did. I blamed her for everything.

"I don't hate you anymore," I blurt out. Crap. The words are falling a little too hastily from my lips, which means I should slow down on the liquor. "I mean, I'm glad we did this, and I think we can be really good friends. You seem like a great woman, and I can tell my brother really loves you."

Danica's bottom lip pouts out as she touches her hand to

her chest. "I love him too. And I don't blame you for being upset, but thank you for giving me a chance. Pull out your phone, and we can swap contact information. That way, you can call or text me too."

I dig my phone out of my purse and exchange contact information as the bartender appears again, pointing toward the upside-down shot glasses.

"We'll take four more," Danica shouts.

I should argue, but I'm not that far from home, and I can walk back if I have to. Maybe this is exactly what I need to rid myself of this low feeling that's plagued me the past few weeks. Because what I thought would be the worst night has turned into some of the most fun I've had in a long time. Danica runs to the bathroom and it takes about two seconds for my brother's most annoying friend to walk up to me.

"Hey there, sexy," Hubbard says, snaking his arm around my shoulder.

"Go away, Hubbard." I fling his arm off of me but he just laughs.

"What is it with you? Always such a snot."

"After all these years, you still don't get that I don't have any desire to do anything with you."

"All I want is a dance."

"No."

Hubbard and my brother go way back. I wouldn't say Hubbard is a bad guy, but he's a player who isn't used to being told no. Which is why I believe he just can't get over the fact that I turned him down on multiple occasions.

"Come on, Holly. Stop being so damn boring."

"I said no."

"You'd like it if you gave me a chance. You have no idea

what you're missing." He drags his drunken finger over the top of my thigh. I grab it and twist.

"Fuck off and don't touch me," I say, staring straight into his lazy eyes.

"Everything okay?" Danica asks, returning to my side.

"Yep," I say to her before turning back to Hubbard. "Go away right now, or I call my brother over here and let him know you just put your hands on me."

He rips his finger out of my grasp and takes a chug of his beer. "You'll change your mind eventually."

"What was that about?" Danica asks, as Hubbard walks away.

"He thinks he's a gift to women and brace yourself because he'll be back. He's relentless when he drinks."

Danica rolls her eyes then orders more shots. I'm already past the point of driving home so I laugh and belly up to the bar.

CHAPTER FOUR

Jaxon

ALL I HEARD WAS Holly saying "no" and "don't touch me" to some motherfucker, and I was in my truck with a heavy foot on the gas, headed straight for Katoka Falls. Her voice was muffled, and from the static and lack of response as I called her name, I'm sure she accidentally butt-dialed me or something. After a few minutes, it hung up on me, and I tried calling her back, but it went straight to voicemail every time. I also tried calling River, but he didn't answer, which can only mean he's out on a fire call for the Katoka Falls Fire Department.

Holly sounded drunk, and the scenarios that are playing in my head are vile as my knuckles turn a transparent color around the steering wheel. It sounded like she was at a bar on the phone, but I don't know for sure. Thankfully, Katoka Falls isn't that big, and I'm fairly confident I'll find her within five minutes of being in town. But if I don't, I'll call Everest,

River's brother, and have his connections track down her phone because I have to know she's safe.

I made it to town in record time, even though it felt like seventeen hours. I pull into Katoka Falls and head down Main Street. There are only two bars in town, and the first one looked empty, so I speed to the other one. Bingo. Full of cars, and the second I turn the corner, Holly's white Bug comes into view, parked on the side of Duke's bar. I park behind it, not giving one shit if the cops come and tow the damn thing. All I care about is getting inside and making sure some son of a bitch doesn't have his filthy hands all over her perfect body.

The heavy door squeaks as I push it open, and the music blares in my ears. An ease flushes the adrenaline out of my veins as I spot the back of her sitting at the bar. I'd recognize her curves anywhere. I'm only a few steps into the half-empty bar when a man staggers up to her, and that adrenaline replenishes when I hear the annoyance in her voice.

"I've been saying no for an hour and a half. How many times you gotta hear it? No. Now, go away."

"Stop being such a prude," the guy says, slurring his words and leaning into her space. "Come dance with me, Jollybug. Now." He grabs her hand, she tugs it away, and I lose my usual calm and collected exterior demeanor.

I grab a handful of his shirt and shove him away from her. One snarky comment out of his mouth and I'll knock him right on his ass.

"You're going to leave her the fuck alone right now, or you won't be able to walk, let alone dance." My voice booms over the music, and he peers up at me, the color in his face draining faster than I can speak. "Touch her again and I break every fucking bone in your body."

"It's okay, Jaxon. Let him go."

"You got a bodyguard now, Jollybug?" He leans around me to look at her and I pull my fist back ready to smash his face in. But I feel Holly's sweet touch on my ribs as she holds onto me from behind.

"First of all," she says, it's not *Jollybug*. It's Junebug, and I never said you could call me that. Second, go sleep it off, Hubbard. If my brother was still here, you would have already been knocked out. Jaxon here is bigger and scarier than Arlo, so if I were you, I'd take off." She shoos him off, and I stand tall, ready to do whatever is necessary for him to get the hell away from her. His eyes flick from hers to mine and then back to hers before he rolls them and walks out of the bar.

"Are you okay?" I ask, spinning around to face her and I wish she hadn't. She looks fucking amazing in a skintight white tank top that shows off just enough cleavage to make me insane.

"What the heck are you doing here?" she asks, ignoring my question.

"You called me."

"No I didn't." Holly doesn't sound as drunk as she did when I heard her over the phone about forty minutes ago, but it's still obvious she's been drinking.

"Where's your phone?"

She grabs her purse from under the bar and starts digging through it. "Dammit, it was in here. Where the hell did I put it?" Her hands begin to travel over her back pockets. I keep my eyes on the back of her head because I think watching her searching every curve may cause me to spontaneously combust. My eyes catch hers as she spins around and flops her arms through the air in defeat. "I don't get it. I had it when Danica gave me her phone number. Then I…" She trails off as her hands brush over her perky breasts.

In a moment of weakness, I allow my eyes to travel down her sexy figure. They stop when they reach an open area of skin between the hem of her shirt and the waistband of her light-wash jeans, where the top of her phone peeks out. It's pressed against her stomach, and now I know for sure she isn't fully sober. I don't know how anyone couldn't feel that.

"It's in your waistband," I say as the music pumps back up.

"Huh?"

I point to it, and she angles her head down, pulling on her shirt and exposing more of her midriff.

"Something on my shirt?" she asks, inspecting it and blocking any view she may have of the phone.

Trying to keep myself an honest man, I turn my head toward the bar, and a man grins as he takes in the sight of Holly and her now bare midriff.

"It's right here," I say, grabbing it from her waistband and tugging her shirt back into place. Her skin was scorching hot, and so was the fucking phone. I'd bet she accidentally dialed me right when she tucked it into her pants.

"That's weird. I don't remember putting it there. Thanks," she says, smiling her usual happy grin and taking the phone from my hand. "Oh my God, it's hot."

"I'm guessing that's how I got called. I overheard you telling some guy to back off, and you sounded like you may have had a few drinks. I had to make sure you were okay."

"Oh my God. Oh. My. God." She smacks her forehead as the pink tint on her cheeks turns a little darker. "I'm so sorry. I am so sorry. You didn't have to come all the way here just for me."

"Yes I did." Her eyes lock with mine and she reaches for me as she loses just enough of her balance to need my arm.

The hair on the back of my neck stands on end as the

electricity from her touch shoots through me. It's the exact feeling I've been dodging since I held her the first time a few months ago. It was easier to deny myself in the beginning. Now I can hardly hear her name without feeling a rush of desire. And by the way she's looking at me, she feels it too.

"Thank you for caring," she says, taking her hands off of me and tugging her long, sheer coat around herself, covering up her hourglass shape.

She sits back down on the barstool and the ice in her glass clanks as she puts it up to her lips.

"What are you having?"

"Coke," she says. "I've been trying to sober up for the last hour so I can go home."

"I can take you home now if you want."

"Um, yes, please. I want to go home so bad," she laughs.

"Do you have a tab going or anything?"

"No," the bartender says, walking up to us. "She closed it a while ago, and we don't charge around here for soda or water."

"That's the way it should be. Good for you." Looks like Duke's might be one of my favorite bars, and I don't even drink in public.

He turns to Holly and taps the bar. "Are you good with him?" he asks her, nodding in my direction.

"Yeah, he's one of the good ones," she says. I'm not sure which one feels better. The warmth in my chest from Holly's compliment or the weight that lifts from my shoulders knowing I'll be able to make sure she gets home safely tonight.

"All right then. You can leave your car here overnight if you want," he says.

"Thanks, Duke. I'll get it in the morning."

He grins at her, nods at me, and walks away.

"Let's get you home, then, Holls."

"Thank God you came," she says, jumping to her feet and swaying just a bit. I grab her arm to steady her as she slings her handbag on her other shoulder. "I wasn't planning on drinking like this tonight."

"Oh?" I place my hand on the small of her back and guide her out of the loud bar.

"Arlo talked me into coming tonight after our chat, and then his girlfriend, Danica, kept feeding me shots. Before I knew it, I had more than a few too many."

I open the passenger side of my truck and watch closely as she pulls herself inside. But my blood pressure is rising by the second.

"Your brother is in there? And he let some dude hit on you like that?"

"No, my brother left already. His girlfriend got sick, and he had to take her home."

"And he just left you drunk at the bar?"

"That was my fault. I'm a little stubborn sometimes and I insisted he take care of Danica. I was going to walk home but then I heard one of the ladies at the bar say her husband caught someone on camera sneaking around their house in the middle of the night. Didn't make me so eager to walk in the dark. So I was trying to get sober enough to drive home."

I shut the door and hustle into the driver's side, start the truck, and head toward Holly's house. I have to stop myself thinking about every horrible thing that could've happened to her tonight. The pushy guy, driving home, walking in the dark. All of it. I'm sure most around this town wouldn't even give walking home at night a second thought. Especially in this small town. But I've lost so much that I can't have the same lackadaisical attitude so many are fortunate enough to have. I was diagnosed with anxiety disorder shortly after my parents died and it's been a full time job keeping my worries and fears to myself.

"I'm just glad I was the one your phone dialed."

In a flash of orange from a passing streetlight, I see her small figure angled in my direction. "Me too."

I park in front of Holly's house, help her out, and walk her up to the barely lit front door. She digs in her purse for a minute and pulls out a very loud set of keys with what looks like a wood bead bracelet attached. After jiggling the door handle for a second, she pushes it open and steps inside.

"I'll go as soon as I hear the door lock."

Her brows furrow as she kicks off her ankle boots and steps to the side. "Absolutely not. You're coming in here too."

"It's late. I better be heading home." *Please, don't do this to me.*

"Jaxon Judge. It is…what time is it?" She turns her head around, spotting the clock, and brings her wide eyes back to me. "One forty-five in the morning. You cannot drive an hour back home now. You'll stay here tonight."

"The drive isn't a big deal. I'm just glad you're home safe. Good night, Holly."

Any additional time spent with her, especially in the space that feels, smells, and oozes her golden aura, will compromise the agreement I made with myself. Holly is off-limits.

"Please, don't go, Jaxon."

Oh no. Not that. Anything but Holly's sweet fucking voice begging me to stay.

"Holly, I…"

"Don't drive all the way home this late. If something happens to you, I'll never forgive myself for making you come all the way to Katoka Falls in the first place. There's animals and probably crazy people on the road, and…and…it would be all my fault."

"Okay," I say, stopping her from going any further. The concern on her face feels like an uppercut to the jaw. I walk inside and close the door behind me, locking it. "I'll stay. But I do have work in the morning."

"So do I," she says, running a hand over her face. "Okay, you can take my bed, and I'll take the couch."

"Woah. I'm not sleeping in your bed." My mouth becomes drier than the Atacama Desert and I move toward the couch. For someone who has been known to be a fairly stealthy guy, I nearly fall over the small ottoman in front of her living room.

"I'm serious. You're like eight foot tall, and that couch is maybe five foot long."

"I'm six foot one, and I'll manage just fine. Good night."

She tosses her purse onto the table next to the door and takes off the long kimono-like fabric, flinging it onto the island that sits between the living room and the kitchen. The soft glow of a kitchen lamp that turned on when she flipped a switch as we walked in surrounds her small frame, accentuating her curves, and I pray she doesn't come any closer.

"Are you sure?"

"Not up for debate, Holls."

Her footsteps are soft as they pad across the floor, closing the distance between us and solidifying that most of my prayers tend to go unanswered. She tucks her tiny body into my core, and instinctively, I wrap myself around her. I breathe her in hoping her scent stays in my lungs, connecting us in the only way possible.

"Thank you for being there for me tonight," she says, squeezing a little harder.

I don't let go until she starts to pull away first. Only when she does, she doesn't go far. In fact, she hardly moves at all. With her arms still loose around my waist, she pauses, and I know better than to look down into her soulful eyes, but I do it anyway. Her feathered, long lashes blink slowly as she smiles and gently pulls her bottom lip into her mouth. *I can't do this.* I have to stop whatever is happening here before it goes too far, and words seem hard to find. So I lean down, put my arm under her knee, and pick her up from the floor. She needs to go to bed and I need to go to the couch.

"What are you doing?" she asks as a belly laugh takes over her, and I realize this is having the opposite effect of what I wanted. I carry Holly down the hall and gently kick open one door. "That's the bathroom," she says, still giggling.

I press another door open with my foot and discover an empty, odd room that isn't big enough for a bed but is too big for a closet. "What the hell is this room?" I ask.

"I haven't figured that out yet either. There," she says, pointing at the last door on the right. "It's that one."

I move to the door and tap it with my foot. Yep. This room is all Holly. A pinkish-orange hue glows from a set of lit crystals in the corner, and a scent of spiced apples fills the air. Wood shelves and macrame hanging pots hold plants of green and yellow. The fluffy cream bedding looks straight out of a magazine and is cool to the touch as I lay Holly down on it. Her hair sprawls out on the pillow behind her head as her playful demeanor disappears, and a sultry grin replaces it. I don't think I've ever seen that look on her before, and now that I have, it's etched into the concrete walls I put around my heart.

"Why are you so damn beautiful?"

Her eyes flare, and she reaches for me. My brain screams

step back, but my heart has a lapse in judgment, and I let her grab onto my shirt and pull my head down to hers. I lean most of my weight onto my arm by her neck as I hesitate, but she doesn't. Holly leans up, presses her soft, gorgeous lips to mine, and I'm a goner. Hers. Forever branded by the woman I've denied myself since I laid eyes on her. Only the slight hold I thought she had on me is more like a vise grip that just keeps getting tighter. The yearning for her spreads from my chest all the way to my fingertips as she tugs and draws me down closer, wanting to get me completely into bed with her. But that's when the faint smell of tequila hits my nose, and I'm brought back to reality. She's been drinking, and even though she seems completely sober in this moment, that is a moral line I will never cross.

I break the seal of our lips, push myself to my feet, and stand next to her bed, breathless, fevered, and completely taken.

"Good night, Holls," I say, running my fingers over her cheek before pulling the comforter up to her chin and heading for the door. I glance back, and that sweet smile I've come to know crosses her face.

"Good night, Jaxon."

I WAKE up to the sound of fast footsteps and shuffling in the distance. I shoot up off the couch, and a ray of bright sunlight hits my eyes. A door slams, and I blink away my fuzzy vision to see Holly running around in a long T-shirt, her hands full of clothes and her purse as she rushes toward the kitchen.

"Holls? What's going on?"

The muscles in my back scream as I take a step. I'm fairly

certain half of my body was hanging over the edge of that couch all night.

"Someone broke into my building."

I'll kill them. I grab my wallet, keys, and phone off the ottoman next to the couch and walk to the door, where my shoes are. Holly passes me before I get them on and flings the front door open.

"Kalina's already there, and…"

"Is Kalina there by herself?" The words fly out of my mouth as I prepare to forgo the shoes and speed to the shop.

"No, River is with her, and they're waiting for the sheriff." She bolts out the door but doesn't get far as I snatch her around the waist and don't put her down until her feet are back in the house. "I have to get to Juneberry. What are you doing?"

I point down to Holly's naked legs. "Pants."

"Shit. I also have no car. God, I'm so stupid."

"That's not happening," I say as she grabs my arm for support as she puts one leg through her pants and then the other. The fact she so casually just put her pants on in front of me as if I've seen her pants-less a million times before, shows how frazzled she is. "You do not talk like that about yourself."

"You're right. I don't. I'm freaking out here though."

"I can see that. But I'm sure River has made sure everything is safe as they wait for the police to show up. So just take a breath for a second, and then I'll drive you."

"You're right," she says, trying to catch her breath. Just when it seems that she's calmed down a little, she smacks herself in the forehead as a rosy color takes over the apples of her cheeks. "Oh my God. Did you just see my underwear?"

"I didn't look," I say, telling the truth and guiding her slowly out of the house, ensuring the door is secured behind us. I follow her to my truck, help her in, and hustle to the driver's side. I may be calm and collected on the outside, but inside, I'm a mixed bucket of anger and worry. Both of which should make whoever broke into Holly's building a scared little mouse.

Holly should be excited about opening her new shop, and instead, she's had nothing but bad luck. Her brother left, and now this. She doesn't deserve all the hell she's getting served lately.

"Jesus. How embarrassing this all is," she says. "And last night. Oh…oh my God. I kissed you last night."

"You regret that?" I ask as we pull up next to River's truck in front of Juneberry.

"No, but I'm sorry if you felt like you had to kiss me back."

I put the truck in park and reach for the handle but pause. "Holly, I wanted to know what your lips felt like on mine the day I met you. I wanted to kiss you the day I held you in my arms at your old shop. I wanted to kiss you at River and Kalina's wedding. I've wanted to kiss you so many fucking times. You just did it first."

I pull the handle and I hop out. River jogs out of Juneberry and up to the truck and he starts talking, I look back to Holly, who hasn't moved a muscle other than her eyes. They are stuck on me as her mouth sits half-open.

"Holly? You okay?" River asks through the open driver's-side door. I hadn't even realized he stopped talking to me. I was too busy absorbing this look of terrified awe on her face.

"Yep," she says, shaking herself out of the trance and hopping out of the truck.

"Someone kicked in the back door of the adjoining shop," River says, leading us inside the store. "Kalina is in with the sheriff, and he's already cleared that side and the store."

"Did they steal anything?" I ask.

"Not that we can tell. They didn't gain access to Juneberry at all. Only the empty shop. The sheriff wants to see your surveillance cameras," River says, to Holly as we walk into Juneberry.

"I don't have any yet," she says. "They're supposed to come put them up next week when they put in the alarm."

"Are you telling me you have zero security here?" I ask, glancing at River, who looks just as unhappy about it as I am.

"I tried. They can't fit me in until late next week." Holly pinches the bridge of her nose. "I knew opening this place was going to be stressful, but what the hell is going on?"

Kalina and the sheriff appear as they walk out from the back rooms.

"Sheriff Anderson," Holly greets him as he tips his wide-brimmed hat toward her.

"Other than the back door of the vacant half, everything else looks to be secure. I'm not sure what's going on around here, but we've got units sticking around town since the car break-ins."

"Is that plural?" I ask. Holly mentioned hearing something about a car break-in last night, but if there's more than one, that spikes a different type of suspicion in me.

"There were about ten. A few people got some footage on their home cameras, but other than body build, there wasn't much to go on. Taking a guess, it could be some kids causing trouble, but we can't be sure. Just keep everything locked up, and call us if you have any other issues." Sheriff Anderson hands Holly what I assume to be a report and tips his hat once more before walking out.

River, Kalina, and I surround Holly as she bites her bottom lip and nervously looks around the shop.

"Holly," River says. "I'm not trying to take over your business decisions, but Kalina isn't my only concern here. You're family to me too, and I can't have your place be vulnerable like this." He pulls out his phone and presses the screen a few times, and I already know exactly what's about to happen. "Everest, I need you," he says into the phone and then walks to the other side of the shop.

"What's going on?" Holly asks.

"You're about to get the family treatment, and if he didn't do it, I was going to," I say. The wide grin that spreads across Kalina's face has me shooting her a "shut up" glare, which only makes her pleased face more pronounced. "This place is about to be safer than a damn fortress."

And that means maybe I'll be able to focus on work during the day instead of whether Holly is safe in her shop or not.

"Didn't expect to see you here this morning, Jaxon," Kalina says, lacing her arm with Holly's. "Did you just drive in?"

Holly giggles and lets her head fall into her hand as River walks up and taps me on the shoulder.

"Can I talk to you?"

"Gladly," I say, following River to the other side of the room as the women walk together to the counter, where I'm sure Kalina is prying any info she can out of Holly.

"This isn't good, is it?" I ask.

"I don't like this damn vibe I'm getting around here. Something is off, and I can't put my finger on it."

"I agree. Why would someone kick in the door to the empty room and not even try to get in here? Doesn't really make sense."

"That's exactly my thoughts. There's no evidence they even tried to get into the adjoining door to access Juneberry. Is it possible it's just some bored teenagers? Sure. Do I feel like it is? No." River sighs. "I've got someone coming to fix the door today, and Everest is coming to help me install a security system tomorrow. The car break-ins are one thing, but now breaking into a business seems like…"

"Like they're upping their game," I say with a growing pit in my stomach.

"Yeah. And they're fucking with our women now."

"Um. Wait a second. Holly and I aren't…"

River puts his hand on my shoulder. "I know you. Probably better than anyone on the planet next to Steph. That," he says, pointing to Kalina, "is my woman. And that…" He slowly pans his finger to Holly. "That's yours. Whether you want to admit it to yourself or not. And someone just kicked in her door. Which means we need to do something."

"If you think I'm not raging inside right now, you're wrong." I tilt my head, desperate to feel a release of the tension from my shoulders to my neck.

"Nope, that's pretty much exactly what I thought. Go look at that back door, man. It's fucked. Until someone gets caught, we're going to have to be vigilant. I'll be around most of the time, but Kalina and I are heading to her parents' in a few days. Just so you know."

"I'll be sure to be in town while you're gone. I'll also have a talk with Zayn and Cole just so they know what's going on in case we need them."

"Good. I'll see if Kalina and Holly need anything else before I head back to work. Otherwise, I'll see you this weekend, right?"

With everything going on with Holly, I almost forgot about this Friday night.

"I'll be there. I hope you prepared Kalina. She's brave as

hell having a game night in the house with four competitive guys."

"She can hold her own. And if she has it her way, she won't be the only woman there."

"Fuck. I hate that I have to go back to Airabelle Valley. But I have a load of projects I have to finish."

River grins. "It's fine. I'm here and you know I'll have my eyes on both of them every second I can. I'll let you know if I think you need to come back."

I pat River on the shoulder and walk to Holly.

"Do you need anything before I go?"

"Nope. Kalina said she'll take me to my car, and other than that, I'm good. Thank you so much for being here though."

"Always. I'll see you later." She nods, and I turn to Kalina, giving her a quick, friendly hug. "See you this weekend, Kali."

"If not sooner," she teases.

Her giggle fades as I walk out the front door of Juneberry and around the building. My palms sweat as I see the exterior door with huge dents in it and the frame totally busted. I walk inside, and my footsteps echo in the space that's identical to Juneberry but lacks the brightness of Holly's touch. There's nothing in here. Why would someone go through so much trouble for nothing? Something definitely doesn't add up around here, and until I find out what it is, that distance I swore to put between Holly and I is now non-existant.

CHAPTER FIVE

HOLLY

A BELL CHIMES above the front door of Juneberry as Kalina walks in. My eyes float from her to one of the cameras that I always feel is aimed right at me. Everest, River's brother, came three days ago, and they hooked up one of the most excessive security systems I've ever seen.

"Hello," she sings as she makes her way over to me with two cups of coffee. She stops at my side as I'm folding one of the sweatshirts from a local screen printer with our logo on it and follows my eyes to the camera. "Something wrong?"

"I just feel like I'm being watched all the time."

"They wouldn't do that," she says, handing me one of the cups. "Unless they think there's a reason to check them, none of the guys are going to just watch the cameras."

"I know, and I trust them. Otherwise, I wouldn't have let them put them in. I've just never had cameras inside the store.

At my old shop, they were only on the outside. It will just take some getting used to."

Kalina's shoes clank on the wood floors as she walks around, sipping her coffee. I tip the warm cup back and close my eyes, and the chai tea latte with a shot of espresso comforts my soul.

"Well, I think it's for the best. Especially after talking to Berta at the coffee shop."

Berta owns and runs Katoka Coffee Co., the best coffee shop in Georgia, and she's been a constant comfort to me since my parents moved out of town years ago. However, she also runs the biggest rumor mill in the entire southeast. "What now?"

"Apparently, Elijah told her someone vandalized Arlo's old shop. Another vacant building."

"If that's true, this is getting nuts. Thank God Arlo doesn't have his rock shop there anymore. But maybe they are just kids and being dumb in the vacant buildings."

"Maybe. But it's got River on edge. Other than when he's at work, he's been stuck like Velcro to my side."

"Yeah, Jaxon has been texting me a few times a day asking me if everything is okay."

"Speaking of Jaxon..." Kalina starts, and I immediately turn away from her. She's my best friend, and I tell her damn near everything. But I have no answers other than the ones I've already given her about Jaxon. We are friends, and that is all. "I was just going to ask you if decided to come to game night. I think he'd love it if you came."

Game night. A new tradition Kalina and River are trying to start. I love games, but I can't seem to control myself around Jaxon anymore. I'm not avoiding him completely because after what's happened lately I think that would be impossible, but I'm not sure if a fun evening together is going to pour some cold water on the fire that was stoked the other night.

"We got a few more boxes in today," I say, changing the subject.

"Okay, okay. I give up trying to convince you that the two of you have serious chemistry and that you both deserve to be happy."

"And what if we give whatever attraction we may have for each other a shot and things don't work out?"

"What if they do?" Kalina casually takes another sip of coffee.

"What if someone gets hurt? There's too many people that could be caught in the crosshairs. Like you and River. I can't risk our friendship."

"I understand that thought process, Holly but…"

My phone chimes, and I grab it off the table next to me to see a text from Mom.

MOM: Hi baby! We're passing through Katoka Falls tonight on our way up to North Carolina. Meet for Dinner at Simon's Steakhouse? See you at seven!

SAVED BY THE TEXT.

"Looks like I'm meeting my parents for dinner tonight at Simon's. Sorry."

Kalina cocks one eyebrow. "I didn't know your parents are in town."

"Neither did I. That's not unusual though. They blow through here a few times a year." I take a glance around, and my shoulders drop. "I can't wait to hear all of her suggestions for the new shop."

"By suggestions, do you mean criticisms?"

"Exactly," I say, laughing.

"Well, if you want to come after dinner, we'll be up playing until at least midnight. Just keep it in mind. My friendship will never be conditional, Holly. You and Jaxon have nothing to do with you and me. Don't cheat yourself because you're worried about other people. That's not fair to you or to Jaxon."

She flashes me a smile and heads to the back toward the office, which is just a big room in the back of the shop. I try to get Jaxon out of my mind and get to work.

For being only one week away from reopening, I'm feeling pretty good about the progress Kalina and I are making in the shop. Half of the orders I have been waiting on came in yesterday, and we spend most of the day getting them priced, entered into the system, and put out on the floor. My stress levels have finally evened out again, and I'm feeling much more like myself.

"Are you sure you don't need me to stay?" Kalina asks, yawning.

"Absolutely. You better take a nap if you're going to be up until midnight."

"Ha, I wish. I have all the food to get ready since River will be working until the guys get there. Besides, it'll be loud enough to keep me awake. Are you heading out soon too?" she asks, swaying toward the door with her hands full with her purse, lunchbox, and coat.

"I have that meeting with the potential tenant in half an hour, and then I have to rush home to change for dinner. No doubt my mother will have her pearls on, so I sure as hell can't go like this."

"Oh shit. I totally forgot about the meeting. I can stay," she says, dumping her stuff on one of the tables.

"I'm fine, I promise. You have stuff to do."

"It's not a big deal. I can wait so you don't have to be here alone."

"Don't worry. I have eyes everywhere," I say, pointing to the cameras. "I was at my old shop from open to close every day all by myself before you started working with me. I'm fine. Seriously, go."

"Okay, but River is at the firehouse for another hour or so if you need anything. Have a good dinner with your parents, and maybe I'll see you later for a drink?"

"No. If I come, there will be no drinks for me, thank you very much."

Kalina laughs, unlocks the front door, and pushes it open with her butt. "I understand if you don't end up coming, but I hope you do."

"All I can say is maybe."

"That works for me. Bye." She waves and walks out.

I bring an empty box that I just unpacked to the back, put some music on my phone, and start my least favorite job of breaking down boxes. Cardboard cuts are the worst, and it doesn't matter how careful I am, I get at least one every time. Sanitizing my hands anymore is like dipping them into hot lava. But it's one of those tedious things that has to be done before I can recycle them. Kalina got me a long box cutter in hopes that it would help. It doesn't.

"Ouch. Goddammit," I shout.

"You okay?" a deep, raspy voice asks from behind me. I swing around, lose my balance, and fall into the corner of the shoulder-height filing cabinet. The impact of the corner into my chest takes my breath away, and I see the floor getting closer to my face. A hand wraps around my arm and stops me from hitting the ground. Once I've regained a sturdy foot, I spin around to a man I don't know standing in my office. *Shit.* I didn't lock the door after Kalina left, and the music must have drowned out the bell above the door.

"Who are you?" I ask, realizing I still have the box cutter in my hand, so I hold it out toward him. I fumble on my desk next to me for my phone, and he puts his hands up.

"Woah. I'm sorry. We have an appointment, but I'm early. Um, I can go back outside if you…"

Way to go, Holly. "No," I shout, dropping the box cutter and shutting the music off. I swallow hard a few times, trying to rub away the pain in my chest. "I'm so sorry. You just startled me."

"No, I'm sorry. I should've waited in the front a few more minutes. Are you okay?" he asks, running his hand over the thick fabric table runner Kalina put on the top of the filing cabinet. She warned me the corner of that thing was an accident waiting to happen. As always, she was right.

"Yeah, I'm fine. I'm Holly."

"Dusty. Dusty Vilhouer," he says, placing a hand over his chest and flashing me a crooked smile. If I had to paint a picture of what a young woodworker looked like, I would have painted an exact image of Dusty. Peeks of dark hair stick out from the light gray beanie on his head that matches his T-shirt, layered underneath a black-and-red flannel. His tight black jeans feed into black boots, and his scent of cedar and pine wafts in the air. He looks like a young artist.

"Are you sure? You look a little pale. Here," he says,

touching my arm and guiding me back to the chair that sits behind my desk. "I'll get you some water."

Dusty turns to leave the office, but I stop him. "No, please. It's okay. I have to tell you anyway, but someone broke in a few days ago. It's put me a little on edge, but they didn't steal anything, and the door has already been replaced and upgraded. I've also had cameras installed all around the building, so rest assured, it's secure now. Nonetheless, I should have locked up when I was back here alone."

"I heard about that. I had my car broken into outside of my house."

"Oh no, I'm sorry. I don't know what's going on around here lately," I say, pushing my hair out of my face.

Dusty sits on the corner of my desk. "Right? I've been here for a few months now, and it wasn't like this when I first moved in." He glances over at me, and his eyes get wide. "Crap. I'm sorry." He jumps off the desk and starts straightening whatever papers he may have crinkled. "I suck at being professional."

"Good," I say, laughing. "I'd much rather have a super-casual relationship than an uptight one. Go ahead, sit back down." He smiles wide and sits back on the desk. "How long have you been a wood carver?"

"Since I was a kid. I spent the summers with my grandpa on his lake in Tennessee. He was a man of solitude and spent his days either whittling away at sticks or building an entire dining room table. I learned everything I know from him. He taught me a man only needs a few things: a few skills, a few bucks, and a few friends. I'm doing good on the first two. Friends are a little harder to come by these days."

"I know how that goes. Well, let's go check out the space

because I'm already convinced that you'll be great to have next door."

After a quick walk around the empty shop next door, I'm shocked when he has no qualms about the lease and didn't even try to negotiate the monthly rent.

"All I need now is the deposit, and we're all set," I say, grabbing the keys to next door from my purse.

"Hang on a second. I'll be right back," he says, jogging out of my office, and I hear the bell above the front door chime.

What the hell? Did he just ditch and run? I get up from my chair and walk to the office door, which is just a large opening between my office and the front shop. Through the front windows, I see Dusty fumbling through his car. He closes his car door and heads back inside with something in his hands.

"Please do not tell me you left all of that money in a car that was just robbed?" I say, squinting my eyes as if I'm trying not to look.

"Of course not, but I have something for you." He walks closer and hands me an envelope and a wooden plaque. "I didn't want you to think I was trying to bribe you into letting me lease the shop next door, so I waited until it was a done deal."

With my mouth fully ajar, I run my fingertips over the carefully crafted carved wood of a juneberry branch. "This is absolutely gorgeous."

"Thanks," he says, looking surprised to hear a compliment.

"I'll be anxious to see some of your other pieces when you open."

"Well, I'm hoping to be open in just a few days."

"Wow, you're going to have all of your things set up that fast?"

"Come hell or high water," he says.

My phone rings from the desk in my office, and I glance at my watch. "Oh no, I have to get that, I'm sorry. Is there anything else you need?"

"The keys."

"That may help," I say, laughing. I grab my phone without looking at the screen and silence the ringer as I hand him the keys to the shop next door. "Thank you so much for my beautiful sign, and I'm excited to have you next door."

"It was no big deal. I'll be around starting tomorrow."

He gives me a side smile and walks out of my office. I wait until I hear the chime above the door and check the missed calls, expecting to see my mother's phone number there. But it's Arlo, and he left a voicemail.

I walk to the front door, lock it up tight, and press Play.

"Hey, Junebug. Since you're making me check in with you like a child, I'm just letting you know we made it to Colorado. We're heading to Aspen tomorrow to go skiing with Danica's cousins. I would like to know why I have to tell you every moment of my life while you can just ignore the fact that you're hiding a whole-ass boyfriend from your family. And don't even try to deny it. Hubbard told me all about your *friend* at the bar. He also said your Bug was still at the bar in the morning, but your driveway wasn't necessarily empty. All I have to say is it's about damn time you let someone in again. Anyway, we're off to dinner at a fancy restaurant where I have to wear a tie…blech. Love you."

With only a little time to get ready for dinner with Mom and Dad, I save Arlo's voice message so I don't forget to call him back and set the record straight about my so-called boyfriend, and I race home.

I do a quick search of my front yard, porch, and overall house before I feel safe enough to get out of my car and jog inside. I kick my shoes off and immediately trip over them, nearly falling again. I catch myself this time, but all I can think about is how embarrassing that fall at the shop was. *Slow down, Holly.* The world has been spinning so fast these past few months, and there's so much to do that it feels like I'm pushing the gas pedal nonstop. I've been a frazzled mess between the opening of the shop, finding a renter so I can pay my loan, the break-in, and the shock of Dusty walking into my office. Today was a giant wake-up call that I need to be more responsible with locking things up because that could have been anyone.

Taking much slower steps, I head to my bedroom. The casual jersey dress I wore today is too casual for my mom for dinner at Simon's Steakhouse. I put on a pair of black faux-leather leggings and a sleek black tank. Facing the mirror, I run my hand over the space on my chest a few inches below my right shoulder and wince as I think about how it could have been my face that met the corner of that filing cabinet. It could've knocked out all my damn teeth. I shiver at the thought as I pull on an oversized rust-colored duster cardigan that covers my darkening bruise, slip into my suede camel ankle boots, and head right back out of the house.

Mom and Dad burst out of the booth they're sitting in when they see me walk into Simon's Steakhouse. Mom rushes me first and wraps me up in the mom hug I miss so much.

"Hi, baby. Oh, I have missed you." She strokes the back of my head the same way she always does, and I lean into her.

"I've missed you too."

"My turn, Janis," Dad says, pulling on Mom's arms. "Give me my girl."

I move from Mom's nurturing embrace to Dad's strong

one, soaking in all of it before they're gone again. Which, knowing them, is probably sooner rather than later.

Simon's is a local favorite, so it doesn't surprise me to see Berta waving incessantly at me until I notice her and wave back. She looks gorgeous in a layered black dress with a deep red lip and her gray hair pulled back into a chignon.

Mom and Dad scoot close together on one side of the booth, and I scoot into the cold and loney other side. My parents have always been a very affectionate couple, and as I've gotten older, I envy them. I've never had a problem being single until lately. Seems the whole world is falling in love except me. And the thought of that makes the extra space on my side of this booth feel so much bigger.

I shove steak into my mouth as the two of them go on and on about all of their big adventures and amazing things they've seen and done. The stories they have could fill an entire library. But the more they talk, the more confident I become in my decision to stay in Katoka Falls. The constant spontaneous travel is awesome for others, but not for me. I like having roots and comfort in the same routine. But I can appreciate the joy it brings to them.

Mom puts a small piece of tiramisu into her mouth, and I know by the look on her face, the subject is about to change.

"So, um."

Here we go.

"We had a sweet chat with Arlo and his lovely girlfriend this morning."

Oh no. Arlo, you and your big-ass mouth!

"They're having so much fun planning their trips. You should do that."

What? Maybe Arlo didn't say anything. "You know I can't

do that, Mom." I shove a piece of chocolate cake into my mouth and know damn well this conversation is far from over.

"Well, you hired some help now, didn't you?" Dad asks. "Even if it's just for a few days, honey. You should get out of Katoka Falls every once in a while. Broaden your horizons."

"Or maybe," Mom says, setting her fork down and cuddling into dad's side, "there's another reason she isn't leaving. A boy, perhaps?"

Goddammit, Arlo. "No, Mom, there is no *boy.*"

"Arlo said you might have a boyfriend. So…what's his name?"

Dad cocks his head and looks out of the corner of his eye.

"No. There is no boyfriend. I have friends that also happen to be male. That's all. Let's talk about something more fun. Like taxes. Or our latest dentist visit."

"Very funny," Mom says. "I don't know. Arlo seemed pretty convinced you had a new guy. Is it so bad if I wish it was true? I worry about you, honey. You can't let what Ken did…"

Mom means well, but she fails to see how much it hurts every time she brings up my ex-boyfriend. She thinks the burn from his constant lies that broke my heart are still smoldering. They aren't. But I'd be lying if the scars aren't still so visible that I'm reminded every day to never fall into a one-sided relationship again. "I'm not letting Ken do *anything*. I'm fine. I'm happy. I'm at peace. And that is everything I have ever wanted. So please, I'm begging you. Change the subject."

Mom and Dad stare at me for at least forty-five seconds before she sighs, and he tugs her closer into his side. She places her hand on his chest, and he kisses her forehead.

"If that's true, then I'm happy for you," she says.

"I couldn't leave without saying hello," Berta says,

walking up to our table. "It's been a while since you two have been in town. If I'd have known, would have made you up a loaf or two of jalapeno bread."

Everyone that has ever stepped foot in Katoka Falls loves Berta. She makes it so easy with her warm smile when you walk into the coffee shop. During the busy season, it's always packed, and she treats every single customer like family. Especially the locals. The last time Mom and Dad were in town, I'm pretty sure they ate so much of Berta's jalapeno bread that they can't even look at jalapenos anymore.

"Oh, that's so sweet of you. We'll be sure to stop by the next time we're in town. We'll be leaving town tonight."

"Tonight?" I even surprise myself with the tone that came out of my mouth. "You just got here."

"Well," Berta says, looking uncomfortable. "Just make sure you lock up tight tonight, honey." She pats my hand, and Mom gets a curious look on her face.

"Why? What's going on?"

"Oh, ever since they busted into Holly's building, we've all been a little extra cautious." With the speed of a sloth, Dad turns his head my direction. Apparently, Arlo didn't fill them in on everything. A nervous chuckle comes from Berta. "Well, I have to run. So good seeing you again." She turns to me and twists her apologetic face. "I'll see you soon, I'm sure."

"It was so nice to see you again," Mom says. The smile stays on her face until Berta walks out of the restaurant. My mother is a free spirit and has always encouraged Arlo and me to take risks and spread our wings. But she still has a mama bear side, and I know she's about to freak out. "Someone broke into your store? Why didn't you tell us?" she shrieks.

"It wasn't a big deal. A bit unnerving, yes. But they only broke into the vacant part of the building. Juneberry was fine."

"That's a little too close for comfort, honey. I hope you've upped your security."

"Yes, my friends have made sure I have the best system around. Everything is fine. Now, why are you leaving so soon?"

"You promise?" Mom asks.

"Yes. I promise. Everything is okay. The sheriff thinks it's just some bored kids."

Mom settles back against Dad, her shoulders rising with her calming breath.

"We're meeting up with friends in North Carolina, and then we're all heading to Sweden," Dad says.

"Dogsledding," Mom adds with glee, changing her tune from only a moment ago. "We'll be back for a real visit soon though."

A man walking up to the pickup counter catches my eye. *Hubbard.* I hold up my napkin in hopes he doesn't spot me.

"What's the matter?" Dad asks, spinning around to get a glimpse.

"Nothing. That's Arlo's jackass friend, and I thought he was leaving town too."

"Is he giving you a problem?" Dad asks, ready to protect his two favorite women.

"Not since Jaxon threatened to tear his legs off," I say, giggling. I peek over the napkin and see him slip back out without even a glance in my direction.

When I return my eyes to my parents, they're both smiling again.

"He's just a friend."

"Next time we're in town, maybe we'll get to meet your...*friend.*"

Choosing to ignore Mom's last attempt to get any

information I might give her, I get a little excited about having my parents at my new house. "Where are you two sleeping tonight? You can come to my house."

"We got a hotel about an hour from here already booked. That way we don't have to get up so early to leave," Dad says as he puts a bunch of cash into the black bill folder.

"Really?" I ask, disappointed.

"I'm sorry, honey. I promise, next time we'll stay longer. It just didn't work out this time."

"I'm just glad I got to see you at least," I say.

We stand from the booth, gather our things, and walk out of Simon's together. The sun has already set, so Mom and Dad walk me to my car and hug me and tell me they love me. After I'm safely in my car, I watch them walk across the lit-up parking lot, Mom tucked tightly into Dad's side with his arm protectively around her. And even though seeing them like that after all of these years makes me warm inside, it also magnifies this loneliness that has suddenly popped up.

It's been barely a week since Arlo left, and I already miss him. Before Arlo closed his rock shop, I lived in one of the apartments above it, and he lived in the other one right next door. Rarely did I ever feel truly alone. And now, the thought of going back to my dark and empty house only exacerbates that. I start my car, pull out of the parking lot, and drive in the opposite direction of home to Kalina and River's house.

CHAPTER SIX

JAXON

"TELL COLE his cat is a total asshole," Stephanie says, huffing into the phone. "I walked in, and he ran between my legs, scaring the shit out of me, then knocked over a plant and ran through the dirt. I just spent an hour cleaning Cole's fucking house. Tell him I'm charging him a cleaning fee."

My laugh echoes in the hallway at River and Kalina's house. A roar of laughter explodes from the other room, and I'm glad I stepped out to answer Steph's call. "You're the one who agreed to pick up that package from the post office and bring it to his house tonight. We all know that damn cat is the devil."

"It's a good thing he's so cute because that's all Freddy's got going for him. Anyway, let Cole know his package is safely in his house. And just so you know, I'm home for the evening."

"What? No date tonight?" I love this. One less thing taking up space in my brain tonight.

"Nope. I ordered a pizza, and I'm going to watch a movie, drink a glass of wine, and go to bed."

"That sounds relaxing for you. Enjoy and I'll talk to you tomorrow."

"Oh, I will," she says, and disconnects the call.

River, Kalina, Cole, and Zayn all shout in the kitchen, and I jog out to rejoin the group when I spot her. Zayn pulls out the extra chair for Holly, and she sits down at the folding table Kalina set up for game night. Holly flashes a gorgeous smile around the table and then her eyes land on me. She looks amazing as usual but it's her dark red lipstick that has my blood picking up pace through my veins. It doesn't matter what she puts on, she always looks gorgeous. Her petite body is swallowed by a large sweater, but I saw her before she sat down. Tight leather leggings. Is she trying to kill me?

I take my seat across from her as Kalina shuffles the cards.

"I've never played this game before," Holly says.

"What?" Cole asks from next to me. "You've never played Spoons before?"

"Nope."

He gives her a quick rundown on how to play, and Kalina deals the cards.

"Things go real fast," Zayn adds. "Just hand all your good cards to me."

"You better not," Cole shouts and everyone laughs.

"Ready?" Kalina asks, getting a nod from everyone and starting by passing a card to Holly.

The cards go flying around the table, and River is the first to grab a spoon. We all dive in, and Cole, Zayn, Holly, and I all have a spoon in our hands.

"Damn," Kalina says, clenching her empty fists as we all laugh and she marks down her letter.

As the game progresses and the competition heats up amongst us, it's hard for me to keep my eyes off Holly. The simple, thin gold chain around her neck glistens as she bounces around in her seat as she shrieks and laughs. That shimmering aura I've grown to love about her radiates through the room, and I'm captivated. So much so that I completely missed everyone reaching for a spoon.

Laughter erupts at my loss and Holly gathers the cards in front of her when the sleeve of her sweater knocks a few to the floor. Zayn leans down to pick them up and as soon as his head is above the table, he raises his eyebrows at me. He knows I always go for a win and that I was highly distracted by Holly. I roll my eyes at his head shake and glance down at River, who is giving me the same knowing grin.

"Woah. What happened to you?" Cole's tone pulls me from the playful silent banter with his alarmed tone. I follow his line of vision across the table to Holly as she pushes her large sweater off, revealing a large, fresh bruise on her chest. But it's the marks on her arm that have the devil stealing the air from my lungs.

"What the fuck is that?" I ask, my heart racing and tingles shooting through my hands as I ball them up into fists in my lap. The room falls silent, and all eyes are either on Holly or me.

"How did you do that?" Kalina asks, tugging Holly's shoulder back so she can take a better look at her chest.

Zayn, Cole, River, and I all shoot out of our chairs at the same time. Zayn lifts Holly's arm to get a better view as I round the table to get a closer look myself, hoping it's not what I think it is.

"Oh, that," she says. "I fell earlier and…"

I reach Holly, and Zayn passes her arm to me. "This isn't from a fall, Holly. Who did this?" I raise her arm to get a better look, and a tremor rattles through me as the marks look like someone grabbed her.

"I'm trying to tell you, I fell, and Dusty grabbed me and—"

"Dusty? The guy who you had an appointment with today?" Kalina asks.

Keys jingle from the kitchen, and Cole already has on his shoes.

"Where is he?" I ask, dropping her arm and heading toward the door. I don't need any fucking shoes.

She jogs toward me, grabbing the side of my shirt and jumping in front of me.

"Let me explain, will you?"

The fire from Holly's hand on my chest stops me in my tracks as she searches my eyes. I take a breath and nod.

"Okay, Holls. I'm listening."

"I was in my office and got distracted with my music as I was breaking down the boxes. Dusty came in, but I didn't hear him."

"You didn't lock the front door when I left?" Kalina asks from behind us. I glance at my three friends, who all look ready to end someone right alongside me.

"I forgot. Anyway, he showed up for our appointment and accidentally scared me. I turned around and fell into the filing cabinet."

"I told you that thing needs to be moved to the back of the office," Kalina says.

"That doesn't explain the marks on your arm," I say, digging my fingernails into my palms.

"Well, if you saw how I ricocheted off the filing cabinet and was heading face-first to the ground, you would've grabbed my arm to stop me too," Holly says, running her fingers over the discolored skin on her upper arm. "He probably saved me from impaling myself on the damn box cutter I had in my hand. I would tell you if someone hurt me, I promise."

Cole pinches the bridge of his nose and kicks off his shoes. "So, you're saying no one hurt you then?"

"That's exactly what I'm saying. It was just an accident."

"All right," Cole says, patting my shoulder. "She's good, man." Cole turns and heads back to the table.

Zayn walks away and grabs something from a bag on the couch. He returns with a tiny bottle and hands it to Holly.

"Put two to three drops on your bruises a few times a day, and they'll be gone before you know it."

The temperature in the room lowers as they all return to the table, leaving Holly and I by the front door.

"What is this?" Holly asks, inspecting the dark brown bottle.

"I have no idea, but I bet it works. He has a fix for everything." She giggles and tucks it into her hand. I can't seem to find my humor at the moment. "Are you sure you're all right?" My fingertips graze her arm, and goose bumps pepper her skin. Her perfect skin.

Holly steps into my space, right where I like her, and angles her sexy eyes up at me. "I promise."

"And this Dusty guy?"

"He apologized profusely for startling me and seems really nice. You can meet him the next time you stop by the shop and judge for yourself. But please, just trust me on this."

I do trust Holly. What I don't trust is someone I don't

know. People can be experts in deceit. The muscles in my jaw burn from being clenched for so long. She lowers her head, and the loss of her eyes feels like someone just ripped a Band-Aid off my arm, hair and all. Putting my finger under her jaw, I gently lift her eyes back to mine. "I trust you, Holls," I whisper. The natural glow returns to her face as the wrinkles in her forehead disappear. With my finger still under her chin, I draw her close. She tips up on her toes, meeting me halfway, and I place a soft kiss to her ruby lips. It's the only thing that calms the gnawing worry inside of me. The brief kiss is enough to make me forget where we are. But it only takes a second after our lips have parted that we both realize there's an entire room that just witnessed that. And every one of them is grinning from ear to ear.

"Should we just try to pretend that didn't happen again?" Holly whispers as we look in the direction of all of our friends, who have quickly turned back to the table, pretending they didn't just see it all go down.

"First of all, if you think they aren't going to be all over this, you're mistaken. And second of all, absolutely not. We kissed. I feel better. You?"

"Yep." She laughs under her breath. I'm not even sure she realizes that she's playing with the hem of my shirt, but it's driving me wild and putting even more images in my head that weren't there two seconds ago.

"Good. Do you want to go play another game?"

She nods, drops my shirt, and walks back to the table. It takes me an extra second to turn around because I would have given anything for her to say no and demand we leave right now... together.

After a few hours and multiple games later, I'm shocked no one has said a word about the kiss. Cole lost two rounds, and I think that was our saving grace. Everyone was too busy giving him shit and gloating about beating him that their attention was taken off Holly and me. But my attention was not distracted from her. I watched her all night and didn't even try to hide it. Her eyes darted to mine all evening, too, as she unconsciously tormented me with her gorgeous smile and contagious laughter. Watching her interact with my friends and fitting in as if she's been part of us from the start only makes me want her more. I'm not sure how much longer I can deny how much I like her. How much I *want* her.

Zayn stands from the table, stretching, and Cole does the same, signaling the end of the evening.

"It's after midnight. I can't believe you guys are going to drive all the way back to Airabelle Valley tonight. You know you can stay here," Kalina says.

"I have things to do in the morning," Zayn says. "Plus, I've got an energy drink in a cooler in the back seat." Cole yawns, and Zayn playfully punches him in the stomach. "And a blankie for the baby over here."

"It's not my fault you like to blast the air-conditioning when it's thirty below," Cole says.

"At least you don't have to listen to that all the way home," River says to me, gripping my shoulder and laughing. I would have ridden with Zayn and Cole, but I was still finishing up a big job at work when they wanted to leave. Besides, I'd rather drive myself and be in control.

River and Kalina walk us all out onto their front porch.

"This was fun," Kalina says. "Don't forget, everyone, Jaxon has game night next month. Then Cole and then Zayn."

"I've already got it all in my calendar," Zayn says.

Holly turns to Kalina. "You two have fun this weekend at your parents' house. Tell your mom I said happy birthday."

Kalina pulls Holly in for a hug goodbye. "I will. And please, for the love of God, keep the front door locked when you're working tomorrow. I feel bad I'm leaving you until Monday with only a few days until opening."

"Don't worry, lessons were learned today. And do not feel bad about going to your own mother's birthday party. I'll be just fine," Holly says, tugging her sweater tighter around herself. "I appreciate you all letting me come play tonight. We'll see you later."

"Stop right there," Cole says. "Let's not act as if you aren't coming next time. You're coming to all game nights too, Holly."

"I thought you knew this," Kalina says, snuggling into River's side.

"Whether you like it or not, you're stuck with us," Zayn says, tapping her arm. "Don't forget to put that oil on. At least twice a day and definitely tonight."

She nods. "Then it's only fair that I host a night too. Throw me on the schedule."

Zayn pulls out his phone and taps on the screen a few times. "Okay, you're in the month right after me."

"Got it," she says, grinning, and the guys give her a quick big-brother-type hug before Cole and Zayn walk to their truck.

"You two be careful going home," River says. He winks at me and guides his wife back into the house. I follow Holly to her white Bug, not knowing exactly how to end this night. She covers a yawn as she opens her driver's-side door.

"You going to be okay getting home?" I ask, grabbing her door and waiting for her to get in.

"Oh, yeah. I'm not that tired." She twists her sweater in her hand and pauses in the crook of the door. "What about you? Are you going to be okay driving all the way home?"

"Of course." I run my hands down her arms, lean in, and kiss her. But it isn't the kind of kiss I want to give. It's the short, sweet, and respectable type of kiss you give on a first date. Her eyes sparkle from the moonlight and she bites her bottom lip.

"Good night, Jaxon."

"Good night."

I hold the door as she slips into the driver's seat. She gives me a sweet smile, I close her door, and head to my truck. I follow her until we reach the outskirts of Katoka Falls where I usually turn down a back road that winds around town to head home from River and Kalina's house. I feel the distance grow between us as I lose sight of her taillights through the trees and I can't stop this yearning to turn around. Every moment I spend with Holly feels so right, and the further I get from her in this moment, the more wrong I feel. A gravel driveway appears to my left, and I slam on my brakes and use it to do a U-turn. Holly is already walking up to her front door before I catch back up to her.

I haphazardly park along the road in front of her house, jump out, and take a few steps into the center of her yard, where I stop. I don't know what I was planning on doing once I got here. I know what I want to do, but pushing Holly into anything she's unsure of isn't going to happen. Hell, even I have a small reservation about getting too close to her now that she's a full participant in my tight-knit group of friends. She stares at me with her mouth half-open, looking shocked that I'm even there, and then without a word, she carefully takes the steps, unlocks her front door, and pushes it open.

"Come in," she says. Powerless to her demand, my feet can't take me to her fast enough.

"I don't have to if you don't want…" Her mouth crashes

harshly onto mine, and I lose all ability to keep my hands to myself. I snake my arm around her waist, and she jumps into my arms and wraps her legs around my waist. Her fingertips dip into my hair as her lips part, and our tongues collide. I kick the front door shut with my foot and swing her around, pressing her up against it as I bolt the lock and kick off my shoes. I hear hers hit the floor behind me, and she works off her sweater, which falls to the ground as I move her from the door. Her desperate grasp around my neck tightens as my hands cup her ass, holding her against me. That trepidation I had earlier? It was just put to a cold and gruesome death.

CHAPTER SEVEN

Holly

I break the kiss only to pant, "Last door on the right." Jaxon chuckles and wastes no time carrying me down the hall and into my bedroom. He was here before, and I lost control, thinking it was wrong and risky and totally a bad idea. Tonight, I don't give a fuck. For months, I've ignored this cosmic pull that draws me to him. Mainly because I'm so concerned about how it might affect everyone else. Jaxon said himself, sometimes it's necessary to be selfish, and if I want that to be true in any moment, it's this one. I've never wanted anyone more than I want Jaxon right now. We've been playing this game of cat and mouse for too long, and the way his eyes danced across my skin all night had an ache between my thighs that was almost painful. If he hadn't followed me home, I would have kept that to myself and the walls of this bedroom as I moaned his name, like I have many nights before.

He lays me down on the cool sheets and his eyes once

again roam over my skin. Goose bumps rise on my arms and legs as he runs his index finger from my bottom lip over my chin and down the center of my chest. My back arches as my body begs him to take me fast, hard, and feral. The thought of it makes me wetter than I already am, and he cups my breast firmly as he leans down and sweetly kisses my lips.

"Jaxon," I say, breathless. "I need you now."

He runs his slightly open mouth over my jaw and licks the bottom of my earlobe, sending a shock wave of pinpricks through my body straight down to my core. With his knee between my legs, I can't rub them together to ease the greedy desire that grows there, and I think I'm going to go mad. He holds himself barely above me on one arm as his other hand dives under the hem of my shirt, tickling my skin as he slowly pushes my shirt up. I reach for it and attempt to rip the shirt off myself, but in one swift move, Jaxon grabs both of my wrists and slams them above my head.

"Patience, baby," he growls in my ear. "I've been waiting a long fucking time for this."

My mouth falls open, and I'm fairly certain that if I were standing, my clothes would have just fallen off completely on their own. He bites my neck just hard enough to make me whimper and moves my wrists to one hand as the other wanders back down my body. He grabs the elastic waistband of my leggings, yanks it down on one side, and slides his hand in over my naked ass. My chest heaves from excitement as he hikes my ass up to meet the bulge of his erection, and he grinds once against me.

"Holy shit, Jaxon."

He lifts his head and grins as I try to remove one of my hands from his grasp. He lets go and freezes. I take advantage of his release, grab his black T-shirt, and giggle as I try to be as smooth as he is but fail massively.

"I thought you were hesitating," Jaxon says, giving in and helping me remove his shirt. It's not the first time I've seen him without a shirt on, but it might as well be. I take in every curve of his muscled chest and arms as he hovers over me.

"You aren't the only one that's been waiting. And right now, I'm going insane." I run my hand over his firm chest and chiseled abs but have a bigger target in mind. As soon as I reach the waistband of his jeans, he reclaims my wrists and puts me back into the position he wants.

"Leave them up there," he demands and waits for my nod before he lets go.

He runs his tongue over my bottom lip before pressing his hot mouth against mine, darting his tongue inside and easily luring me into a state of debilitating need. The sound of our kiss separating echoes in the quiet room, and my quick, ragged breaths soon fill it as he pulls the top of my tank top and bra down, exposing my nipple and pulling it sharply into his mouth. As he nips, sucks, and flicks his tongue, I can't stop my hips from writhing beneath him, desperate for some sort of relief. He tugs my shirt up, and I lift my back, eager to get the damn thing off me. I want it all off. I want to be reckless. Impulsive. Greedy, even. I take in Jaxon's devious grin as he removes my shirt, works off my bra, and drags them up over my arms. His eyes burn with hunger as he studies my body and shakes his head.

"Fuck me," he whispers, bringing his lips back to mine. He inhales as the peaks of my nipples rub against his chest, and he moves his mouth there, teasing me as if I need to be primed any more than I already am. I close my eyes and tilt my head back, trying to control myself from going over the edge before he's even gotten into my pants. Turns out I don't have to wait any longer as he lowers himself onto his side next to me. His hand dives under the fabric, and he hisses as his fingers slide through the slick heat waiting for him.

I moan into his kisses as he rubs my overly sensitive clit, and I thrust my hips up, trying to get him to push his fingers inside, but he smirks against my mouth.

"Don't make me hold you down, baby."

Oh God. Please hold me down.

I can't form a single sound other than "Oh God." His relentless swirling against my clit brings me to the edge, and I start to beg. "Please," I say and buck my hips. "Please, Jaxon."

He ignores my plea and takes my mouth as my orgasm teeters on the edge, and I sharply inhale. At the exact moment I feel like I can't take any more, he plunges his fingers inside mercilessly as he groans and watches me come undone. My moans turn to ravenous whimpers as he takes his fingers away and scoots off the end of the bed, and about half a second passes before Jaxon has my pants and underwear flying through the air. I hear the rip of a condom wrapper, and I know it's coming, but my body is still electric and unable to hold still.

I feel the bed dip at my feet as he kneels his way between my legs. Expecting to feel the tip of his cock against my entrance, I'm taken aback when his firm, warm tongue lands on my core and laps me up. My thighs squeeze his head as my body convulses, and moans turn to roars of euphoria. I grab hold of his hair and gently tug with the blinding desire for him to be inside of me once and for all. With one harsh suckle, I lose his mouth but gain the tip of him. He presses it barely in.

"Is that what you want, baby?"

"Yes," I pant, reaching for him, but he grabs my wrists once more and holds them just above my shoulders.

"Say it. Say you want me," he says, his voice rumbling as he stares down at me, sucking his bottom lip into his mouth.

My breasts rise and fall as I struggle to take a deep breath. "I want you, Jaxon. I've always wanted you."

His eyes flare and his mouth crushes onto mine as he slowly sinks inside, stretching me to fit him. "Oh my God," I moan into his mouth. "Jaxon."

"How are you...so..." Jaxon slowly pulls out to his tip, releases my wrists, and grabs hold of my hips, then thrusts hard inside as I cry out in sheer satisfaction. "So...fucking perfect?"

"Jaxon," I pant as he continues to pull out slowly and then thrust mercilessly back in.

"You." He pulls out, then drives back in. "Are." Out slow. "Mine," he says, sinking himself deep inside.

Losing my mind and any restraint I have built up, I moan, "I'm yours, Jaxon."

Three words out of my mouth, and the man goes feral. My headboard crashes against the wall over and over again as he makes every fantasy I've ever had about him modest compared to this. My dry throat burns with every sharp inhale and cry out as he works me just the way I needed him to. Jaxon holds a tight grip on my hips as his thrusts quicken and get shallow. He changes his angle and hits the sweet spot that sends me straight to the fucking moon. My inner walls constrict against him as my orgasm paralyzes me. Gripping onto his rock-hard forearms, I dig my fingernails into his skin, just trying to hold on.

"That's it, baby. Give it to me," he says as a guttural groan slips from his chest. He thrusts once more, buries himself completely, and lets out a long groan as I feel the twitch of his erection inside. As he braces himself above me, his hungry glimpses have morphed into satisfied relief. He pushes a piece of hair off my face and slowly leans down to kiss me. His lips are soft and sweet as he caresses my cheek with his thumb. I whimper again as he gently slips himself out of me but keeps his face close as he searches my eyes.

"You realize this is done now, right?" he says, and it's as if someone shot down my favorite glistening star in the sky. My heart feels like it just ruptured, and the damage ricochets through my chest. Panic sets in as I hear his words repeat once in my head. His thumb brushes over my furrowed brow. "There's no going back. Not after knowing how you feel... how you taste. I can never go back to the way it was."

"Me either," I whisper, realizing he wasn't telling me he got me out of his system and was done with me. Relief coats the pain that was taking over a moment ago as he kisses my forehead, then my nose, then my lips.

My legs still shake as he moves, running his hand up my outer thigh and kissing my knee on his way off the bed. He holds his hand out, helps me out of bed, and holds me steady on my feet.

"You okay there?" He proudly grins.

"Never better," I giggle as we walk toward the bathroom.

After a quick cleanup and a snack of chocolate ice cream, Jaxon and I get back into bed. Out of habit, I lie on my side facing the nightstand, and he settles in behind me, wrapping his arm around my body, tucking me in. He kisses the back of my neck, and I relax against him.

After a few minutes of comfortable silence, I can't help but think about what this all means. I take a deep centering breath and blow it out through pursed lips.

"What are you thinking about?"

"What this means."

He trails his fingertips up and down the top of my forearm, so gentle and sweet.

"You don't have to put a label on any of this."

"But they're going to ask…"

"So what? They can assume all they want. It's up to us if we want to share that we're…" Jaxon pauses, and I know he's having a hard time figuring out exactly what we are at the moment. It's too soon to just jump to boyfriend/girlfriend, but we're definitely past friends. "We don't have to say anything about what we are or are not."

"Okay," I say, snuggling deeper into him and yawning as I lace my fingers through his. "But for the record, whatever *this* is, I don't share."

"Oh," he says, with a menacing tone. "Neither do I."

RAYS of light shine brightly through the cracks in the blinds of my bedroom window. Last night was more than anything I could have imagined. Jaxon groans and tightens the hold he has on me in front of him. I feel a kiss on the tip of my ear, and a raspy, deep voice rattles my insides.

"Morning," he says.

"Morning."

I reach to the nightstand to turn off my recurring alarm before it blares its annoying beep. But by doing so, I've pressed my ass into his already growing erection, and a low, deep growl surges from his mouth. As he pulls me tighter against him, he moves his hand up my body, traipsing over my rising and sensitive nipple before closing it gently around my neck and turning my head toward him. He takes my lips long and hard as I start to rock my hips against him.

"Do you have somewhere to be this morning?" Jaxon asks, peppering me with harsh kisses.

"If I did," I pant as he moves his hand from my neck to between my legs, "I'd cancel."

JAXON OPENS the door for me and I step into Katoka Coffee. I can't describe the feeling of home that comes over me as Berta greets us with her usual cheery face.

"Good morning," she says, her eyes dancing between Jaxon and me before settling in on me. "Would you like your usual to go, or are we having a seat?"

"I think we'll sit in here today."

She reaches into the glass display case and pulls out the last chocolate croissant she has and puts it on a small white plate. I order the same thing almost every day with little variation because her chocolate croissants are my favorite. But everything Berta bakes is to die for.

"Do you have any of those little cheese danishes today?" Jaxon asks and gets a huge grin out of Berta.

"That depends. Are you asking as an out-of-towner or as Holly's boyfriend?"

I pop my hip and cross my arms. "Berta! You better knock that off," I say, trying to hide my smile at her tease, and only get her loud cackling laugh in return.

"Like I don't already know," she says, turning away from us and disappearing into the back.

"I knew Berta was going to say something," I say to Jaxon, smacking my forehead. "Sorry about that."

I jump a bit as Berta pushes open the swinging door from the back, and it bangs loudly against the wall. Jaxon has his hand laced in mine before I can blink.

"I just happen to have a fresh tray," she says, walking over to the glass case and sliding the tray full of cheese danishes in. "How many would you like?"

"I wish I could eat them all, but I'll take two, please."

Berta puts two cheese danishes on a small yellow plate and pushes both plates toward us. Part of the reason I love Katoka Coffee so much is Berta's eclectic taste. Nothing in here matches, and it's absolute perfection.

"Coffee?" she asks.

"Yes," Jaxon and I say in unison. Neither of us got much sleep last night, and any energy I may have naturally produced overnight was depleted again this morning.

Jaxon and I sit along the window overlooking Main Street of Katoka Falls. I finish my croissant and have only a few sips left of coffee when I notice Jaxon staring in the direction of Juneberry, which is just across the street and down about a block. He barely blinks as he takes the last bite of his cheese danish.

"Looks like your new tenant isn't wasting any time moving in."

I look over my shoulder at Dusty getting into an old red truck that looks like the ones that show up on all the Halloween décor in the fall. A second later, the truck rumbles past the large windows and out of sight.

"That's good. He seems pretty eager to get open. I am too but I'm so nervous. There's still a lot to do."

"I'm sure Kalina being gone this weekend doesn't ease your nerves."

"Of course not, but it's okay. I have to get through my head that no matter what gets done or doesn't, I'll still be able to open my doors. All I can do right now is put on some music and work until I'm exhausted."

"I can come back later this afternoon and help you get some things done."

"Oh no, I can't ask you to do that."

"You didn't ask, and let me put it a different way. I'm going home for a while, and then I'll be back with dinner."

I wish there was one more bite of croissant to stick into my mouth to hide the giddy grin I can't keep to myself.

"Would you maybe want to stay another night?"

"Another night in your bed, huh?" he asks, raising one eyebrow and licking the drop of coffee from his bottom lip.

"I mean, only if you want to. I just figured you have to work this week, and then I have the reopening next weekend. We probably won't see each other for a while."

Jaxon sets his coffee cup down and narrows his dark eyes at me. "First of all, I'll be here for the reopening celebration next Friday. Second of all, I will always want to be next to, on top of, or below you in bed."

My belly fills with butterflies as I think about what tonight might hold for me. But right now, I have to get to work.

"That's going to give me something to think about while I'm working today."

"Do you really still have that much stuff to put out on the shelves?"

"I have things coming in every day, but mostly, it's a lot of the tedious things. I double-check everything I did the day before and make sure it was entered into the system correctly, pay the bills, update all of our social media, and since I just reopened our online shop, there's a ton of orders to prepare and package up to ship out on Monday. Plus, there are a bunch of holes in the walls from the previous owners that I wasn't able to cover up with artwork. So I need to fill, sand, and paint."

"And that's just what you want to get done today?" he asks, looking at his watch.

"Totally doable," I say, taking the last swallow of my coffee. "But I better get on it if I'm going to get most of it done by dinner."

Jaxon stands from the table, and I follow his lead. We put our dishes in the brown bin Berta puts on the far end of the counter for dish returns and turn toward the door. "Hang on, I want to confirm my order for the reopening with Berta."

I jog up to the counter, and Berta flashes her eyes to Jaxon waiting for me by the doorway before she leans over the glass.

"Stop it," I say, grinning knowing he can't hear us. "Are we all set on the pastry trays for the reopening celebration on Friday?"

"I will not stop it, and yes we are. River has brought his pack of hotties in here a few times before, and I always knew that one had his eyes on you."

"And how did you know that?"

"Because anytime they were here, his eyes always seemed focused toward your shop."

"Well, we don't know what's going on between us yet, so how about you keep that friendly information to yourself for now."

Her head flinches back slightly. "Why are you hiding it? You both look so happy sitting over there."

I put my arms up on the glass and rest my chin on them. "I'm scared it could ruin everything. I'm here all alone now with Arlo gone, and if I get on the wrong side with Kalina, and River... What if I lose the only friends I have?"

"Nope," Berta says, shaking her head. "That's not how you

make a decision that could affect the rest of your life. You have the biggest heart in the world, Holly. But you can't avoid a good thing that could change your entire future because of the fear of upsetting someone else. You deserve someone with a heart that matches yours, and that," she says, nodding her head in Jaxon's direction, "is a good man. Did you know he found a high school kid with a blown-out tire on the side of the road about six weeks ago?"

"No," I say, confused. "I didn't know that."

"It's true. He not only fixed the blown-out tire but bought him four brand-new tires. Who does that?"

"That sounds like something he would do. But if you knew that, how come I didn't hear about it?"

If anything happens anywhere close to Katoka Falls, not only will Berta know about it, but she'll make sure everyone else does too. So why I never heard about this grand act of kindness is a bit confusing because it's the kind of juicy gossip she loves.

"He asked me not to." I flip my hand in the air, and she realizes what she just did. "Whoops."

I laugh because she can't help herself. I push off the glass and walk toward Jaxon, who opens the door for me. "Bye, Berta," I call, waving at her over my head.

"Bye, honey. Bye, muscles," she shouts to Jaxon, and I spin around to see her wink at him, then disappear through the swinging door as it slams again against the wall.

"Muscles?" I ask, failing to hold back my laughter.

He rolls his eyes and chuckles. "I helped her load a wedding cake once into the back of her van. She's been calling me that ever since."

"Oh, I heard about you helping her carry that cake when

her delivery driver called out. But she left out the part where she gave you a new nickname."

Jaxon places his hand on the small of my back as we walk across the street to where we parked our vehicles by Juneberry. I stop next to his truck, and he snakes his arm around my waist and pulls me with enough force for me to slam into his body. He kisses my lips, then my cheek.

"I'll be back later. Text me any requests for dinner."

"I'm good with anything. Something simple that we can eat in bed," I say, lifting my eyebrow and hoping to get a rise out of him. His mischievous half-grin confirms I did just that.

"I can think of one thing." He pecks my lips again and tucks his hands into his pockets. "You've got to go in before I can't leave."

Loving every second of feeling so desired, I add a little extra sway to my hips as I walk up to the front door of Juneberry. As I let myself inside, I turn around to shut the door and hear him mumble, "Fuck, I'm in trouble." He waits until I turn the lock, then gets in his truck and drives away. With my heart floating in a puddle of anticipation, I turn around and get to work.

It isn't long before Dusty pulls up next to my car just outside of the large glass windows and starts unloading boxes out of the back of his truck. Even though I don't know him that well, I still feel a little more comfortable knowing he's right next door. I wait about an hour and pop my head through the adjoining door.

"Dusty?" I call.

"Hey, buddy," he shouts. "Come on in."

I press the door all the way open and step into Dusty's Woodshop. There are no shelving units but folding tables scattered in the room with pieces of wood stacked all over them.

"I just wanted to say hello and be nosey. Honestly, I couldn't wait to see more of your work. It's all so beautiful. But I don't want to bother you too much." I tuck my hands behind my back so I don't touch his expertly carved designs. Wolves, birds, trees all hand carved into thick slabs of wood. Single carved statues of eagles standing tall on a bit of tree branch fill one table in the front corner. I don't know how he does it, but the talent is incredible.

"Thank you, and you're not a bother at all. You can come over whenever you want. I'm just glad you're friendly. My last landlord was kind of a really mean old lady."

"That makes no sense to me. I'll never understand why people work so hard to make everything miserable. Especially when you have to work closely together." Dusty nods and gives me a smile. "I'm glad you aren't that way either or it would have made this even harder. This was supposed to be my brother's shop and I was really nervous about renting it to someone else."

"Oh?" he says, setting down a large hand-carved Santa figure. "What happened?"

I shrug. "He fell in love and decided to go see the world instead."

"That sucks, and I'm sorry. Although, I'm not because now I have this stellar place to work in. I know I'm not your brother, but you can come hang out anytime you want. I will forewarn you though, I'm kind of a dork."

I laugh, and it's the first time since Arlo left that I've felt like buying this building wasn't a mistake.

"I really appreciate that and feel free to come over to my

side too. I better get back to work. I can't wait to see how you set this all up. It's going to be so cool."

"Yeah, this place is going to be perfect. I'm going to have my carving station back here, with my tools all on this wall," he says, flying past me. Dusty's shop doesn't have a big office area like my side does, but it does have a wide hallway in the back that leads to a bathroom and the back door. The adjoining door that connects our two shops is on the right side just after the hallway begins. "And over here," he says, running to the back corner of the store. "Is where I'll have my laser engraver machine to make custom wedding lyric signs. Those are always a top seller since it's done in front of the customer as they wait. They love that."

"And that's what you needed to put the vent in for, right?"

"Right. I found someone to come put that in for me. River, I think is his name. He came by to check if I needed any help. I asked if he knew anyone who could put that in, and he said he could."

"Yeah, I knew he'd be coming to pay you a visit sooner rather than later. He's a close friend of mine and the husband of my best friend, who also works at Juneberry. So you'll meet her too."

"He was a little scary at first, but then he seemed real nice."

I laugh. "Well, prepare yourself because there's three others just like that. They're a bit overprotective sometimes. But don't worry, I'll make sure they mind their manners. And I can't wait until that vent gets put in because I'm dying to see one of those signs."

He taps his chin and moves a few boxes around before grabbing a knife from his waistband and cutting the tape on the top of one of the boxes. He reaches in, pulling out a warm brown block of wood about two inches thick. I gasp as he turns it around and I see lyrics to one of my favorite love songs engraved in the shape of a heart. "That is absolutely gorgeous. Wow."

"Well, when you get married, I'll make you one."

"And on that note, I'll be going back to work now."

He chuckles and unwraps a large nutcracker. "Yeah, I feel the same way about that subject."

I walk to the door leading back into my office and grab the handle, but before closing it, I stick my head back into the room. "If my music is too loud or annoying, just let me know."

"As long as it isn't techno, we're good. Nothing against it, but it tends to make my head throb."

"Seventies and eighties greatest hits?" I wince, expecting him to roll his eyes.

"Fucking crank that shit," he says, grinning.

"Should I leave the door cracked?"

"Duh."

"Done," I shout and head into my office, leaving the door cracked.

I crank my usual station, and "I Want to Dance with Somebody" comes on. I turn it up and laugh hysterically when I hear a very high-pitched and terrible voice singing along with the lyrics through the door. Yep. This is going to work out just fine.

The day flies, and before I know it, it's already starting to get dark outside. I already put a coat of compound on all of the wall holes around the shop earlier so they would be dry. I'm hoping to get it all sanded and maybe even get a touch of paint on them before I leave for the day. I climb my ladder and press the sandpaper onto the dried compound but the moment I start rubbing the wall, my ladder starts to shake, and I yelp.

"What are you doing?" Dusty asks, running over to me. He puts one hand on the ladder and his other on the back of my calf to steady me.

"I still don't know how they sold me this ladder with good conscience." I look down to Dusty's concerned face.

"Well, get off of there before you fall and kill yourself."

He doesn't let go of my leg as I go to take a step down, and a slow, heavy knock comes from the front door. I spin around, almost falling again as Jaxon stands like a massive statue outside. He doesn't catch my smile because his eyes are focused on one thing. Dusty.

CHAPTER EIGHT

J AXON

THE SIGHT of another man's hand on any part of Holly feels like an entire hornet's nest got knocked down inside of me. I watch while sharp stings attack my chest as he holds the rickety ladder steady, and she climbs down. My eyes stay glued to his as Holly jogs across the room, unlocks the door, and lets me in.

"Hey," she says, greeting me with a sweet tone I hope she doesn't give anyone else. I place a quick kiss to her lips, then take long, slow strides toward the nervous man. Holly jogs to get in front of me. "This is Dusty." Dusty holds his hand out and waits for me to reach him. "Dusty, this is Jaxon."

"Nice to meet you," he says. I shake his hand, but really, I'd love to squeeze it until I hear a few good pops for touching her. "I'll get back to work and leave you two."

"Thanks for running over," Holly says to him. "The last thing I need is to break a bone right before opening day."

"I hear that," he says, then takes a step closer to her and eyes me. "Is he one of the three?" I'm not sure if he even attempted to whisper so I wouldn't hear it. Holly nods and giggles. "I guess two more to go. Watch that ladder, will ya?"

I keep my eyes on him as he walks into the back and through the adjoining door.

"What's wrong with your ladder?" I ask, moving to it and barely putting my hand on one of the steps before it wobbles. "Holly, what the hell are you thinking climbing this thing?"

"It's the only one I have. I bought it from a garage sale like three years ago. I just haven't needed it until now."

I check my watch and know there are about ten minutes before the hardware store in town closes.

"I'll be back."

"Where are you going?" she asks, running after me.

"Stay off that thing, and I'll be right back."

All I could think about to and from the hardware store is how I've wasted time denying my feelings for Holly. I could have lost her to another guy at any point because of my own stupid fears. Judging from the way Dusty was checking out her ass on that ladder, I'm sure he finds her attractive. Who wouldn't? But somehow, I'm going to have to control myself so I don't chase Holly away right from the start. I despise the fact that he had his hands on her. But also, if they weren't, she might have fallen and gotten hurt.

I wish she would have just waited for me to come back, and I could have climbed the ladder myself. But Holly is a strong, independent woman, and I will never try to put out that fire no matter how much it worries me. What I will do is make sure she has what she needs to keep kicking ass without getting hurt. I pull back up to Juneberry, unload the new ladder, and smile at Holly as she opens the front door, shaking her head.

"Jaxon," she says, walking after me as I set the new ladder up next to the old one and take the old ladder down. "What are you doing now?"

"Taking out the trash." I carry the old, dilapidated wood ladder through Holly's office and out the back door and toss it into the dumpster behind the building.

As I come back into the shop, Holly is up on the new ladder, sanding away at the wall. She pauses and looks down at me. "Thank you, but I need to pay for this. How much do I owe you?"

"Nothing. Consider it a gift for reopening the store. It was for my benefit anyway."

"And is that because you're afraid I'll fall or because you saw Dusty holding on to me?"

"Pft." The sound vibrates my lips, making them tingle. "I'm not worried about that kid."

"Oh, well, that's good to hear. Because if I had to guess by the look on your face earlier, you looked a bit…"

"Worried about you falling? Yes, I was."

"I would call it a bit more like, murderous."

Damn, I guess she saw that. She takes each step down carefully until she's eye to eye with me.

"Thank you. And don't worry, I can handle myself."

"You better be the only one handling anything on your body. Other than me, of course."

Sexy isn't even the right way to describe the laugh that comes from her as she places her hand on my chest and I lean in and kiss her. The sandpaper she had in her hands falls to the ground as she cups my head and parts her lips, inviting my tongue to play with hers. For so long, I was able to refrain from touching her, and now that I have a taste of Holly, I'll crave her forever. A noise from the other side of the wall reminds me we aren't alone, and I make sure she's balanced on the step of the ladder before taking a small step back.

"Well, you don't have to worry about that. He reminds me of Arlo. So please, be nice to him."

"All right. I'll try," I say, letting out a long, slow breath. "Now, what can I do to help?"

"I just want to finish sanding. I was hoping to get a coat of the touch-up paint on too, but I'm so hungry I'll just do that tomorrow."

I grab a piece of sandpaper from a pile of them on top of a plastic sheet protecting her products from the dust and start on the spots I can reach without the ladder. Which ends up being most of them. "What did you have for lunch?"

"Nothing. I got so busy I didn't eat."

"Are you telling me all you've had all day long is a chocolate croissant?"

She crinkles up her nose, and it could be the cutest thing I've ever seen her do. "Maybe," she says.

"I thought we could just do pizza, but maybe we should pick up something more substantial from Simon's."

"No," she says, stepping off the ladder and moving it to another place on the wall. "Pizza is perfect."

Between Holly and me, we get through the sanding in no time. She turns off her music and holds the door open that leads to Dusty's Woodshop.

"See you later, Dusty," she shouts.

"Hey, Holly?" She stops, closing the door, and Dusty runs into view. "Can I borrow that ladder?"

"You don't own a ladder?" I ask him, suspicious he just wants an excuse to use hers.

"I had one that a buddy of mine borrowed and never gave

back to me. I was going to go buy one, but it would be sweet if I could use yours for the time being," he says, turning to Holly.

"Have at it," I say, motioning to the back door. "It's in the dumpster."

"Jaxon," Holly scolds, pushing the door open a little wider. "Sure you can. It's over there, but I'll need it back tomorrow. If you aren't going to be here, I can just go into your shop and get it if you don't mind that."

"I have some other things to do tomorrow, but you can go into my shop whenever you need to. I trust you."

Holly may see Dusty as a harmless guy who reminds her of her brother, but I can read him like a book with extra-large font. And he definitely isn't looking at Holly like an innocent sibling.

He smiles at Holly, grabs the ladder, and heads back through the door. "See you later."

"Bye," Holly says, closing the door and turning to me with her arms crossed tightly around herself. "What was that about?"

"Nothing," I say, shrugging.

"You said you'd be nice to him." She drops her arms and walks over to me, grabbing her purse from the desk next to us.

"I said I'd try."

She takes a step toward me, pressing her body hard against mine as she hovers her mouth just far enough away to prevent contact.

"Try harder," she whispers, then turns and walks away. "Let's go. I'm starving."

She shuts the lights off, even though I'm still standing in the room trying to wrap my head around how much she turns me on before quickly walking after her like a dog on a leash. She twists the dead bolt, pulls the door open, and the cool air hits my face. I wait by her side as she locks it up and sets the alarm with her phone before I walk her to her car.

"You like just pepperoni on your pizza, right?"

"Right. I'm surprised you remember that."

"I remember everything about you, Holls. I'll go pick up the food and meet you at your house."

"That sounds good, but can you get breadsticks too, please?"

"You can have whatever you want."

"Pizza, breadsticks, and you is my entire order," she smirks and sinks into her car.

I stop her door from closing, lean in, and crush my lips against hers. Hearing her say she wants me is something I've only dreamed of before last night. It's the only thing I couldn't buy in this world and what I thought was out of reach. Her lips part, and I dive my tongue inside, kissing her with the intense passion she awakened in her office. The desire to have her builds to a point that has me weak, which means I need to go get this damn food and get back to her as soon as I can. She's breathless when I let go and close her door. Her light blue eyes are an inferno as she watches me walk around the front of her car to my truck. But they have nothing on the bubbling volcano ready to overflow in my own chest. I wait until she backs out, and I head to get the food.

Saturday evenings at the only pizza place in town was probably a bad idea. Especially being that I'm in one hell of a hurry now. Liberty's Pizza is packed, and I'm leaned up against the wall, waiting for our order, when my phone rings. I pull it from my pocket and see Cole's name on the screen. I wish I could ignore it, but my anxious mind would never let me get through even five minutes without feeling the need to call back to make sure something isn't wrong.

"Hey," I answer.

"Where are you? I tried going to your house, but you aren't home, and you're not at work. Are you okay?"

"Yeah, I'm fine. What's up?"

"Zayn is dragging me to a scary fucking movie tonight. It's one of those special midnight shows, and if I have to go, then so do you. Meet us at the theater at eleven thirty."

"I can't," I say, squeezing my eyes tightly. "I'm not home, but I think you can handle it."

"Have we met? I most certainly cannot handle it. The last time he made me go, I almost had a heart attack. I'm going to need your first responder training if I have any chance at survival."

I laugh and memories of volunteering at the Airabelle Fire Department with River and his dad, Rick, flow in. It wasn't that long ago but feels like decades.

"I'm sorry, I can't. But Zayn will be fully prepared for whatever catastrophic event might occur with you this evening."

Cole sighs into the phone. "Where are you?"

Shit, here we go. "Um. Not in town."

"So what town are you in?" he asks snidely, and I immediately know that he knows.

"One that isn't that far from Airabelle Valley."

"Does it possibly rhyme with Patoka Malls?"

I can't stop my chuckle. "Rings a bell."

"Jaxon?"

"Yeah," I respond, knowing that our plan of not being open with the others is going to fall apart before it even begins.

"River and Kalina are gone until tomorrow night."

"Yep."

"Which means you're not with them. So how is Holly?" he asks, and I swear I can hear the smile on his damn face.

"She needed some help at Juneberry, and since Kalina is gone, I helped."

"Jaxon, your pizza order is ready," the woman behind the counter shouts, and I know damn well Cole heard that one.

"And you're picking up pizza and won't be home to go to the movie. Okay. Got it. Well, tell Holly I said hi. And if I don't live until tomorrow since you won't be there to resuscitate me, tell her I said it's about damn time that you two got your heads out of your asses."

"Goodbye, Cole."

"Later," he says, and I disconnect the call.

After paying, I put the food in the truck, drive over to Holly's, and race up to the door. Before I can knock, she pulls it open for me. She took *get comfy* to heart and looks so fucking gorgeous in light brown wide-leg sweatpants that cling to the bones on her hips. The matching shirt is cropped and hugs her breasts just enough for me to spot the perked-up nipples through the fabric. It looks soft, and I want to put my hands all over it. All over *her.* But something has changed in the way she's looking at me. She forces a smile as she steps aside, making room for me to pass by her as I walk into the house.

"Everything okay?" I ask as she shuts the door.

"Thanks for going to get the pizza. I'm starving," she says without answering my question. The odd vibe in the room doesn't fade as she takes the pizza and breadsticks from my hands and walks into the living room, placing them on the coffee table. "I grabbed us two beers when I heard your truck pull up." She plops down on the couch and tears the box open.

All those nice cozy thoughts I had only a few seconds ago

when I pulled up are shot down like it's duck hunting season. Something happened between the time I left Holly to now.

"I'm going to pass on the beer. Do you have any water?"

"Oh my God." She jumps up and grabs both beers from the coffee table. "I forgot you don't drink. I'm sorry, I don't know what I was thinking. I'll get us a few bottles of water from the fridge."

Her sudden panic worries me. "Stop," I say, stepping in front of her.

I take the beers from her hand and head toward the kitchen to swap them out for waters. As I pass the island to the fridge, I notice a check written out to me lying next to a burning cinnamon candle. It's made out for the amount I spent on the ladder earlier. She must have looked it up online and found the price. Maybe if I pretend I didn't see it, she'll forget about it. I grab a cold bottle of water from the fridge and watch her carefully as she sits back down on the couch and grabs a paper plate from the table.

"What is going on?" I ask, sitting back down next to her.

"Here." She snaps out of whatever faraway thought she was in the middle of and hands me a paper plate. "And there's a check on the counter for you. For the ladder."

All of my alarm bells are set off, and I don't know whether I need to hug her or go find whoever put this look on her face and kick their ass. I set the plate she handed me down on top of the pizza box.

"Okay," I say, taking her plate and doing the same. "The ladder is a gift, and I'm not moving another muscle until you start talking. You seem distant, and that is completely different from how I left you. So what happened?"

She swallows hard, and I swear her eyes turn a different shade of blue. The sadness nearly brings me to my knees.

"I don't think I can do this," she says, her voice trailing off. The ache in my chest starts low and spreads all the way to my throat. I focus on staying calm even though it feels like the oxygen is being sucked out of the room. She stands from the couch and begins to pace across the living room "I think we want two different things, and I just know I'm going to be the one with the bleeding heart at the end. No matter how much I wish I could keep this connection between us fun and lighthearted, tonight I realized I can't do that."

"Woah, woah, woah. Hold on." I place my hands up, desperate for her to stop talking. Even the thought of breaking Holly's heart makes my stomach churn and puts a sour taste on the back of my tongue. "Explain how we want two different things."

"I was racing around here to freshen up before you came back. I took off my jewelry to put lotion on my dry hands, and when I went to slide this ring back on my finger," she says, twirling the gold leaf ring she always wears on her left middle finger, "I accidently put it on my ring finger instead. Reality kind of punched me right in the face, and all of my dreams that I've created for myself flipped through my head like an old movie. I like you too much to let you break my heart, Jaxon."

"Holly," I try to stop her, but she spins on her heel and keeps going.

"I want a white house with a black picket fence that surrounds a yard big enough for my kids to run. Did you know that?" She spins again on her heel continues in the other direction. "Big diamonds are gorgeous for some people, but I always pictured a simple gold band."

"Holly." I adjust myself on the couch as I watch her wrap her arms around herself.

"I want to host Christmas every year around a huge tree

and spend Valentine's Day with my husband on the floor in front of the fireplace as we sip champagne from flutes we haven't used since the last Valentine's Day."

"Holly, please," I say again, but it's like I'm not even in the room.

"I want to sit in a rocking chair with my grandkids on my knee on the same front porch my kids played on."

Done with the way she's torturing herself, I rise from the couch and step in front of her before she can pace another lap. "Why are you telling me all of this right now?"

"Because you don't. You don't want all of those things. Obviously, we just started this *thing*, but I can't just give myself to you knowing that no matter how my feelings might progress, those things will never come true with you."

"And how did you come to that conclusion?" I ask, my palms starting to sweat as the thought of losing Holly before I've had her in my hands for even a minute kicks all of the fears I worked so hard at hiding into overdrive.

"River told Kalina that you have no desire to ever get into a serious relationship or have a family. That you're happy alone and as an uncle."

I nod. "You're right. I did say that, and I meant it." Holly's entire face drops as she hears the words fall from my mouth. Taking her hand, I lead her to the couch, and we both sit down again. "I said that after a bad breakup. I don't want to talk about an ex-girlfriend, but it's important to fully explain. We were together when my parents died. I changed that day. The thought of losing anyone else scared me after I lost them. I became overprotective of everyone I cared about. And overbearing."

Holly's face twists. "It makes sense that you would."

"My sister understands because she lost that day too. But it didn't take long before I drove my ex away. She said I smothered her to death. Exact words. And it's true. I'm painfully aware of the fact that I'm a lot to deal with. Who wants to be constantly questioned on where they are or who they're with? No one. But, it's not out of wanting *control* of where they go and who they spend time with. I just need to know how to find them."

"Jaxon," Holly whispers and reaches for my face, but I take her hand and hold it in mine. My stomach churns as I spill all my secrets to this woman. This woman who holds my damn heart in her hands no matter how hard I fought it.

"I was fresh out of high school, and watching some movie in my room. It was late, and my phone rang. I could hear the pain in my mom's voice as she struggled to speak." Holly slowly moves a hand to the bottom of her throat as she looks at me like she's afraid to hear what's next. This is exactly what I don't want, but I'm too far in to stop now. I focus on Holly's light pink nail polish as her other hand tightens around mine. "She was coughing and sobbing with what little breath she had left. Somehow she managed to whisper, "Accident" and "Love you," and then there was nothing but a hissing noise in the background. I ran to grab Stephanie, but she wasn't home, and I couldn't get it out of my head that she might be in the car with my parents. I called 911 but had nowhere to direct them. I drove everywhere I thought they could be, trying to find an accident. Trying to save them. It was before our phones had GPS, and I didn't even know if they were in Airabelle Valley. I eventually found the wreck in the country just outside of town, but it was too late. I was too late."

I glance up at Holly, and tears are flowing down her cheeks. This isn't how I pictured tonight or any night with her would go. I haven't rehashed that night since it happened, and the pain feels like a million knives stabbing me repeatedly.

"I'm so sorry," she says, putting her other hand on my knee.

"That's not why I'm telling you this. I don't want you to feel bad for me. I just need you to understand that I thought after my relationship failed, it was pointless to ever get involved heavily again. That anyone I dated would feel smothered or that I'm trying to control them when in all honesty, I'm just... I just get..."

"You get scared," she says.

"Something like that. I had no idea where Stephanie was, and I went insane until I knew she was safe."

"I understand," Holly says. "That's why you drove all the way here when I accidentally butt-dialed you."

"I can't help it when it comes to the people I care about. It's just always been easier being on my own."

"Right." She takes her hand out of mine, and my body screams on the inside, wanting her touch back so badly it hurts.

"Here's the thing," I say, taking her hand back and pulling it up to my lips, kissing it before scooting closer to her. "I have no intention of ever hurting you, Holly. I said those things long before you. From the moment I walked into Juneberry with River, I knew you were going to be different. That I wouldn't be able to ignore how you make me feel and I've never wanted to explain this to anyone before. Now, this is all new to me and a little too soon to be thinking about weddings and such."

"Yeah," she says, nodding incessantly. "Way too soon. But it has to be a possibility for this to go any further."

"I haven't felt this way for anyone other than you. I don't know what the future holds. But I'm not completely closed off to the possibility. But knowing what you know now, do you think you can handle someone like me?" I ask her, leaning in and placing a kiss on her cheek as she lifts one eyebrow.

"Oh, I know I can handle you, Jaxon Judge."

I laugh and relief floods through my body. I hand her the plate back. "You need to eat first." She takes a big bite and relaxes back into the cushions of the couch. "Are we okay now?"

"Yes. I'm sorry you had to tell me all of that to get your point across," she says, taking another bite.

"I didn't. But now that you know, I'd love to not talk about it anymore. Zayn, Cole, and River know not to bring up the past, and there's some things they don't even know."

"I won't say anything. But thank you for telling me. It makes a little more sense about how you reacted to Dusty earlier."

"No, that's just because he had his hands on what's mine."

She takes another bite of pizza as I dig out a slice of my own. "So you meant it when you said I was yours last night."

"If it comes out of my mouth, I mean it. But if you have any doubts, hurry up with that pizza, and I'll show you."

My phone rings, and my heart hammers in my chest as I rush to answer it. Seeing River's name come up on the screen this late creates a lump in my throat.

"Riv?" I answer, trying to sound calm.

"Where are you right now?" I know every different tone Zayn, Cole, and River have, and I can tell whatever he's about to tell me isn't going to be good. Which means I'm not messing around and not telling him.

"I'm with Holly." His deep sigh sounds like static through the speaker. "What's wrong?"

Holly straightens her back and shoots a worried glance at me.

"Elijah just called me." Elijah is the town asshole, but he works with River at the fire station. For him to call River on his weekend off with family, something bad must have happened. "They found Berta in her apartment. She's dead. Someone fucking killed her."

CHAPTER NINE

HOLLY

JAXON SQUEEZES my hand as we pull up to Juneberry. I haven't been able to stop the tears from free flowing down my cheeks since I found out about Berta last night. But the sobbing came as we passed the unusually dark windows of Katoka Coffee.

"I can't believe it," I say through an uncontrollable sob. "I just can't fucking believe it. Who would want to kill Berta?"

"I told you I didn't think it was a good idea for you to come to Juneberry today, and I stand by that. Let me take you home."

I shake my head and unfasten my seat belt. Jaxon insisted on driving me to the shop and staying with me for the day. I didn't argue, but I can't just sit at home and do nothing all day. I need distraction and a goal to focus on. Being at Juneberry is the only way to keep my mind from thinking about her poor kids. Berta has three sons and a daughter and I can't imagine how devastated they must be. She didn't deserve this. A glance out the window to the nearly empty street and the whole town seems lifeless as the rain falls gently. It won't be long before the crowds fill these streets again, but nothing will be the same without her here. It hasn't even been twenty-four hours, but the last I heard, there was still no lead at all about who might have done it. It looks like a robbery turned murder, and it will completely rock this town.

Jaxon hops out and rushes around the truck, but I get out before he can reach the passenger side. He grabs my hand and leads me to the front door of Juneberry as big water droplets fall onto my face. I shut off the alarm from my phone before tucking it back into my pocket, put the key in the dead bolt, and push the door open. Jaxon's hand tightens on mine as he powers into the store like a detective going into a crime scene, looking down every nook and cranny in the place. It isn't until he looks through the office and checks the back door that he lets me go.

I sit down at my desk and turn on my computer.

"I'm going to walk through the shop next door since he already gave you permission to go in there. I'll grab the ladder too."

"You don't have to do that. I'm sure it's fine," I say, knowing that things around here are anything but fine right now.

"That's not how we're going to go through this. You need to be extra careful until they catch whoever is responsible for the crimes happening here. And I will be making sure you're safe."

Wiping the tears and rain from my cheeks, I give him a smile and nod. My chair squeaks as I lean back, waiting for any new orders to load. "Oh my God," I say, looking at the numerous orders I have to package up today.

"What?" Jaxon asks, running into the room.

"Sorry, I just saw how much work I have to do today."

Jaxon lets out a breath, goes back into Dusty's Woodshop, and reappears with the ladder in his hands. He slams the door shut and flips the lock.

"Where's the paint? I'll do that while you handle your orders."

After giving him the paint, I sit back down and attempt to focus, but all I see is Berta's smiling face over the glass counters as she pushes my chocolate croissant to me. Unable to keep it together for even a moment, I flop onto my desk and cry. Berta was one of the few people I could turn to when my parents decided to leave me here in Katoka Falls. I could always count on her to be at the coffee shop when I needed her advice or even when I didn't, but she gave it to me anyway. It's a bizarre feeling that she's just gone. There's no closure. No goodbyes. No final life advice. And now her killer is out there just roaming the streets.

"Aw, honey," Kalina says, letting her purse fall to the floor as she rushes into the office and to me. "I'm sorry it took so long to get here."

I stand from my chair, and Kalina crashes into me as we fold each other up in a tight hug. "I thought you were supposed to be at your parent's house until tonight," I say, sniffling.

"I'm where I need to be."

Kalina and I separate when four men walk into my office. Jaxon, River, Zayn, and Cole stand in front of us, each one with their arms crossed firmly on their chest.

"What are you two doing here?" I ask Cole and Zayn.

"We're here to help. Put us to work. What do you need us to do?" Cole asks.

Kalina threads her arm through mine at my side and rests

her head on my shoulder as we look at the four loyal and amazing men in front of us.

"You guys came all the way here to help me?" My emotions are running high, and the tears start falling again.

Zayn moves from his stoic position among the men and pulls a tissue and a travel-size bottle of aspirin from his pocket. He hands them to me and pulls me into a hug. My eyes shoot to Jaxon, but I don't see a lick of the same reaction that he had when Dusty had a hand on my leg.

"It's what we do," he says, patting my back. "Make sure to give Cole the most annoying job you have."

I chuckle through my tears. "You guys are the best."

"I'm going to help River put in that exhaust next door unless you need me to do something else." Jaxon says.

"That would be awesome, thank you."

Before I can even try to get my brain to function, Kalina delegates tasks to Zayn and Cole, and they hustle out of the office.

"I don't know what I did to deserve all of you. I'd be so lost right now," I say to Kalina once the guys are all out of the room.

Even though my heart is so heavy, I find a way to take a few deep breaths as we work through a few of the online orders. I find calm and peace in the keyboard clicks that echo in a mostly quiet building. Until I hear a voice booming from the front of the shop.

"Who the fuck are you?" Cole's voice echoes through the rafters, and Kalina and I race to see what's going on.

"Talk or die," Zayn says, standing right next to Cole, who has Dusty pinned up against the wall.

"Let him go," I shout. "It's my tenant from next door." Jaxon and River run in behind Kalina and me.

"What is wrong with you just walking in here like that? You don't own this place," Cole says, his lips pursed.

"Stop! He's not a threat. It's okay," I say, rushing up and grabbing Cole's arm. I turn to look for any help from Jaxon to see a grin spread wide across his face. River isn't moving too fast either. "Let him go." Cole finally releases Dusty from the wall and walks toward River and Jaxon.

"With everything going on around here, maybe you should be more careful about just barging into a store that isn't open to the public," Zayn says before he follows Cole.

"Are you okay?" I ask Dusty, who looks scared out of his mind.

"That's all four of them now, right? No more surprise gargantuan going to show up and toss me around like a wet rag?"

Dusty looks over at the guys, who are chuckling in the corner. I sigh but can't deny that I love how protective they are of Kalina and me.

"That's all of them. I'm sorry about that but I think we're all on edge today. I'm surprised to see you though. I thought you said you weren't going to be coming in today?"

"I wasn't planning on it but when I heard what happened to the coffee lady, I wanted to make sure everything was all right here. When I pulled up, I saw those two guys through the window going through the boxes and I thought you might be in trouble."

Oh, bless this guy and his good nature, but I'm not sure what he thought he would do to scare off two men the size of Zayn and Cole. Dusty is petite for a man and doesn't look like the "little but mighty" type. He looks like the "run away fast" type. He's still clutching his chest as River calls him.

"C'mon, Dusty. You can help us put in your exhaust for your machine. Where is that thing anyway?"

"It's at my house. My friends were supposed to come and help me get it in here since it's so heavy. I'll probably just have to hire someone."

River looks at the three guys, and Jaxon's shoulders drop. "Fine. We'll get it," he groans.

"Really? That's awesome," Dusty says, trotting past the four men that make him look like a toddler next to them. Kalina giggles and blows River an air kiss. Jaxon winks at me and follows Dusty and River over to Dusty's Woodshop.

Cole and Zayn go back to work unpacking the stack of boxes that I didn't get to yesterday and Kalina and I head back to the office to finish up the online orders.

"With all of this help, I might get a majority of this stuff done way before we reopen."

"That's what they're hoping for," Kalina says. "I heard River talking to Jaxon on the phone this morning. Jaxon has to go back to Airabelle Valley for work this week, and he is not thrilled about you spending any amount of time in the shop alone."

Dusty sticks his head through the adjoining door. "I didn't know the coffee lady was a close friend of yours," he says, stepping toward me. "I just overheard your friends talking about it. I'm so sorry." Dusty pulls me in for a hug, but the moment his arm drapes around my shoulder, Jaxon steps in through the doorway.

He strides to Dusty, grabs the back of his shirt, and pulls him off me. "Easy, Jaxon," I say.

"That is the second time now I've seen your hands on my woman." His tone is low and deep, and I swear I see Dusty shaking. "Be a friend, that's fine. But keep your fucking hands to yourself. I see a third time and I'll roast marshmallows over the bonfire I make from all your pretty wood plaques in there."

"Jaxon," I warn.

Kalina snickers at my side, and Dusty takes another step away from me as Jaxon pats his shoulder. "There you go, Dusty. You're getting the hang of it now. River needs you to show us where you want the switch on the wall."

He laughs nervously and speed walks out of my office.

"He's scared shitless. You guys are going to run my tenant out of my building, and then I'm going to have to claim bankruptcy and close down Juneberry," I say to Jaxon.

"Like I would ever let that happen," he says, snaking his arm around my waist and pulling me in for a kiss. I flash my eyes to Kalina and then back to Jaxon's, and he grins. "I think she knows already, Holls." He places a chaste kiss on my lips and lets me go. "And don't worry about Dusty. Guys just need boundaries, and I think he got all of them made clear today. He'll be all right now."

Kalina laughs as Jaxon leaves the office, and I look at her with wide eyes. "They're going to kill that poor guy."

"Nah," Kalina says. "River kind of likes him."

"Really? He doesn't act like he does."

"I can't explain how those guys work. Besides, what we should be talking about is how Jaxon just made you two official."

Heat rises in my cheeks, and I know I'm probably blushing. "He's been so sweet." Guilt for forgetting about Berta takes hold of me, and I tear up again. "Especially since last night. He just held me and let me cry all over him."

"If anyone knows all about loss, it's him," Kalina says, sitting in the chair and scooting up to the computer. "Anyway, let's focus on these online orders and not the heartbreaking reality outside of the shop, okay?"

She knows I have to work on something to keep my mind distracted. And with opening day only five days from now, there's no more time to waste.

JAXON WALKS THROUGH MY HOUSE, checking every window and door, some more than once.

"And you'll set the house alarm after I leave?" he asks.

"Yep. I promise." Hopefully, I can remember the code. My landlord gave it to me before she went to Florida for the winter but I've never even thought about setting it until tonight.

"I hate leaving you here right now." Jaxon pulls me into his arms, cups my face, and swipes his thumb over my cheek.

"I'll be okay. River already told me if I need anything that he'd be here in five minutes, and the sheriff assured the town that he has extra units coming in from county. I'm more worried about you driving home so late."

"I'll text you when I get there," he says, sighing before taking my lips with his. The long, deep kiss goes straight to my heart. "I'll be back on Friday for your opening but if you need me for anything before that, one call and I'm right back here."

"Will you stay with me on Friday night?"

"Absolutely."

I sink into his warm embrace, breathing in his scent until he loosens his hold on me. "I'll wait for your text. Be careful driving home."

"You know I will. Bye, baby." He kisses me again, then walks out the door. I can tell he doesn't move from it until he hears the lock engage. I move to the alarm on the wall and set it.

It's been a confusing few days. Last night, I thought Jaxon and I were already over. Then he showed me a vulnerable side of him I hadn't seen before. The relief I felt when he explained everything to me was like a kind of euphoria. Then the world came crashing down again with the news of Berta. This is the shittiest roller coaster I've ever been on, and I want off.

———

WITH THE OFF-SEASON of Katoka Falls still in swing, I wasn't sure there would be a crowd at Juneberry's reopening day. But there was a handful of people waiting outside of the door for me to open. A few are familiar locals, but most of them must have come from the awesome signs that Jaxon made for me in his graphics shop to hang around town.

"Ten minutes," Kalina shouts from the office, and River rushes to set the stack of cups next to the three drink dispensers each filled with ice water flavored with different fruits. The cucumber-and-mint-infused water is my favorite and reminds me of the one time I went to a spa with my mom. I've had to stop myself from drinking it all before the doors even open.

I've been anticipating this day since I closed the doors at the old shop. Even though my nerves about buying my own building have been tested multiple times, as I stand here and look over the gorgeous, light, and airy place that fills me with joy, I couldn't be more proud of myself. But I also know there's no way I'd be where I am without my friends.

"Holly," Kalina shouts. "The tablet for the register just froze."

Like a swift kick to the gut, my stomach falls as I race to see if I can fix the problem before the doors are open. I put my finger onto the screen, and the cursor moves.

"It's all good now. Maybe it's that lotion you just put on." I pick up the jar and look for the nonexistent label. "What is this stuff?"

"Take a whiff," she says, grinning.

I inhale the scent of cherries and almonds. It's Kalina's signature fragrance. "Did you make this?"

She nods. "I'm still trying it out to see if it's good. I guess not when you're trying to work the register though."

"We can hardly keep your hand soaps in stock. They're going to go nuts over this stuff."

"I hope so," she says. "I've been making a mess at home trying to perfect it. Pretty sure River is about to kick me out."

"Not a chance in hell," River says, coming around the corner. "I'll take you and all your mess." He kisses her cheek as he passes us with a handful of flowy, dark gray maxi dresses on hangers that came in yesterday and I left in the office. He knows his way around this shop almost better than I do at this point and I couldn't be more thankful he's willing to help out.

The alarm on my phone buzzes in the back pocket of my jeans, and I shriek. "Finally." I race to the front door and open it wide.

"Welcome to Juneberry," I say as a group of people walk inside, and their "oos" and "ahhs" fill my soul with more oxygen than all the plants in the world.

Amongst the familiar faces in the crowd is one that I've become particularly fond of. Jaxon strolls in with a bouquet of unique light pink flowers. Flutters and twists fill my stomach as he comes near and wraps his arm around my waist.

"Happy reopening, baby."

Pressing up on my toes, I kiss him. "That is so sweet." He hands me the flowers, and I put them up to my nose and take a big whiff. Nothing.

"I don't do well with floral scents, and my sister told me about these. They don't have a strong smell, but I thought you'd like them."

"I love them. What are you doing here so early though? I thought you were in the middle of a project and wouldn't be here until later."

Aside from the hundreds of text messages that Jaxon and I have been exchanging every day since he left last weekend, we've spent every night before bed on the phone. Especially the night Sheriff Anderson announced they had a suspect under arrest for the murder of Berta. The man was also suspected in the car break-ins. They caught him trying to break into the hardware store in the middle of the night but by the time morning came, it was all over so there wasn't too much fuss about it. Other than the collective loud exhale of relief from the entire town. And especially from Jaxon. I could tell in his voice how relieved he was to hear someone had been caught. Even though he still told me not to let my guard down, there's been a difference in his tone ever since.

"I finished early and gave the other project I had today to one of my guys so I could be here when you opened."

I kiss him again for being so sweet and he follows me through the store as I get a little giddy watching my customers shopping again. We walk through the large open doorway into my office and I grab the large square glass that I always use as a candy dish from my desk and a pair of scissors to get the flowers into some water.

"Holly," Kalina calls from the front. "I need you up here."

Jaxon takes the scissors from my hand and shoos me away.

"Go ahead. I'll take care of this." Just before I leave the office, Dusty walks through the adjoining door. Jaxon holds up the scissors with a sinister grin, and Dusty yelps, much to his delight. "I'm just kidding," he says, chuckling and snipping off the first stem.

"You're a funny man, Jaxon," Dusty says, pretending to chuckle too. But there's panic in his face. "Did you happen to flip the breaker at all?"

"What do you mean?" I ask, my heart starting to pound from being pulled in two different directions.

"I have no electricity in my shop."

"Oh no," I say, moving toward the door that leads into Dusty's Woodshop. Dusty had been determined to open as soon as possible and has been open for a few days already. From what I could tell through the windows, he's been pretty successful already at getting people through the door. I can't wait to see how busy he gets when the tourists start coming back. But not having electricity is a huge problem and since I own the building, it's my problem.

"Holly, there's an issue with the internet connecting," Kalina says, jogging into the office. "I tried calling, but they told me they couldn't help me because my name isn't on the account."

River comes in behind her with a pillow from Handcrafted Harvest in his hands. It's his day off from the fire station, and he's choosing to spend it at Juneberry helping. I didn't think we were even going to need him, but I couldn't be more relieved that he's here now. "There's a hole in the corner of this pillow, and a customer wants to know if there's a discount on it if she buys it."

Even though I expected there might be some glitches, I

hope this isn't an omen of how the rest of the day is going to go.

"You go take care of that stuff, and I'll figure out why Dusty's power is out," Jaxon says.

I nod, and everyone takes off in a different direction. Except me. My feet seem to be stuck to the floor as I try to wrangle my overflowing emotion of appreciation. It wasn't long ago I thought I was going to be completely alone. Now, here I am with a best friend, four guys that would do just about anything for me, and a boyfriend. *Wait. What did I just say?*

"Holly?" Kalina peeks her head into my office, and I snap out of it and jog out of my office.

Many hours later, Cole, Zayn, River, Jaxon, Kalina, and I are sitting around a large round table in the middle of Simon's Steakhouse. With my roasted garlic chicken fully demolished, I relax back in my chair, sipping sweet white wine as Jaxon's hand pulses on my thigh while he laughs at something Cole said. Today was full of surprises. There were a few kinks in the system that got worked out, but mostly, I was just so taken aback by the support the people at this table showed me today.

I catch Zayn looking at me from across the table. With narrowed eyes, he twists his head and mouths, "You okay?"

Unable to stop the yawn, I cover my mouth and yawn while I nod in response. "I'm just so thankful for all of you. I can't believe you all came."

The conversations at the table get quiet, and Cole leans his elbows onto the table. "We wouldn't miss a big day like this. You worked your ass off, and the place looks amazing."

Zayn nods. "The place kicks ass, Holly. You two did a really good job."

I glance over to Kalina, who put in just as much work as I

did, and she beams with pride, but the only response I can find is another yawn. Jaxon pats my leg and rises from the table, with everyone else following suit. He already fought with Zayn and River about the check and won, paying for all of our dinners.

"Thank you all so much for coming. Seriously, I love you guys." I hug Kalina, and she clutches me back tightly. "You've worked so hard. Thank you."

"We make a great team," she says. "I'll be in at nine tomorrow."

"Is there any way you can come in at eleven instead? I have a few things I need you to do after we close tomorrow, so it might be a little later than usual."

"Sure," she says, shrugging. "But I don't mind if you need me to be there all day. River is working anyway, and I went a little crazy with the lotion experiments that my racks at home are overflowing."

"How about this? If I get super busy, I'll call you. Otherwise, just come at eleven."

"Okay. Have fun tonight," she says, wiggling her eyebrows and glancing at Jaxon as he jokes with the guys next to us.

"Yeah, you too."

Zayn, Cole, and River hug me goodbye, and Jaxon walks me out to his truck. I feel like I haven't slept in a century. The constant worry about today has lifted from my shoulders, and now I'm just exhausted, and judging from the way Jaxon helps me into the passenger seat, it must be evident all over my face.

"C'mon, baby. Let's get you home."

The few-minute ride across town to my house lulls me into a comfortable daze, and I can only assume it's the same comforting feeling a baby gets right before they fall asleep in the car. Jaxon parks in my driveway, and it takes so much effort just to get into my house. I let everything in my hands fall to the floor and worry about picking it all up in the morning. We kick off our shoes, Jaxon takes my hand, and he leads me down the hallway and into my bedroom.

We had plans for tonight. I had been telling him all week long how I couldn't wait to get him back into my bed, and now I feel as useless as a wet sock on a rainy day. He reaches into the bag he brought, pulls out a pair of silky athletic shorts, and tosses them onto the bed. I grab a sexy silk nightgown from my drawer, and Jaxon gasps as he lets his jeans fall to the ground.

"Is that what you're wearing to bed?"

"Yeah," I say, another yawn taking over.

"I think you're trying to kill me. You've had an extremely long day and you need some good rest. But, I haven't felt you next to me in a week and that's your nightgown of choice?" He sighs.

I laugh and pull my shirt off over my head. "Sleep is overrated."

He grins then angles his eyes to the ground as I stand before him. "What time do you have to be at the shop in the morning?" He slides his shorts up his legs and tugs off his shirt.

"We open at nine, but I need to get there about an hour earlier. Why?" I eye him seductively as I reach around, unhook my bra, and let it fall to the floor.

Jaxon lifts his eyes to my naked chest and shakes his head as he moves around the bed. He grabs my nightgown and slides it over me. The cool fan blowing a slight breeze onto my skin makes me shiver and my nipples peak. I shimmy off my tight white jeans, and Jaxon lifts my comforter for me to get in. He shuts the light off and climbs into bed next to me. I reach for him, and instead of cupping my breast or kissing my neck, he pulls me in close and wraps me up in his arms. The abundance of comfort he gives me has me drifting within minutes.

"I'm sorry I can't follow through with all of those dirty things I texted you about," I mumble, yawning and getting the best chuckle from him.

"We'll have plenty of time for all of that when you aren't so exhausted. But tonight, baby, you need sleep."

I snuggle into the crook of his neck, and he turns and kisses my forehead. "Are we still…unlabeled?" I ask the ridiculous question that makes me feel like I'm in high school, but at the moment, I can't think of a better way.

"Holly, we haven't been. You're my girlfriend. I'm your boyfriend. We're together. You're mine. I'm yours. That's it." He lifts my chin and kisses me with a level of adoration I've never felt before. "Good night, Holly."

DO I SMELL BACON? I turn and find the other half of the bed, where Jaxon was last night, empty. Noises of cooking and silverware being set onto plates come from the kitchen, and I smile. Then I freak the hell out and flip over to check the time. My plan was to leave the house in forty-five minutes. I bolt out of bed just as Jaxon comes through the door with the tray that usually sits on my coffee table and holds the remote controls.

"Get back in bed. You're ruining my special moment here. I know you need to get going, but not before you eat."

I jump back into bed as instructed, and Jaxon places the tray in front of me, then walks back out. "Wait, aren't you coming to eat some of this?" I look at the full tray of food.

"I need to go clean up. If you saw the mess I made in

there… just do me a favor and stay out of the kitchen until I clean it up a little." He runs his hand over his dark brown hair as he grins and I melt inside at how sexy he looks in the morning.

"I could care less about anything in the kitchen. Come kiss me."

He saunters over to me, cups my cheek, and I taste the coffee on his lips as he kisses me deeply. I sink my hand into his hair and give it a little tug but he smiles against my kiss and slowly backs away.

"Tonight, you are all mine." His sweet expression turns hungry and dark in all the right ways. And suddenly, I can't wait for this day to be night. He pecks my lips once more than heads out of my room.

I devour what I can of Jaxon's sweet breakfast in bed and get ready for work. Even though he came into my room without a shirt, I still wasn't prepared to see Jaxon's muscular back standing at my kitchen sink as he washes dishes. His shorts sit low on his hips, and I can't help but watch him for a moment as each muscle in his back contracts and releases as he moves. This is every woman's fantasy right here.

"Do you dry them too?" I ask, wrapping my arms around him.

"And put them away."

"Ohh," I whimper, acting turned on as hell as I giggle. He spins around, snatches me up, and sets me on the counter as he pushes himself between my legs. My breath is stolen from my lungs as he crushes his lips to mine, showing no mercy as he plunges his tongue inside. His erection presses against the material of my dress that got caught between us, and any shred of acting has been decimated. I *am* turned on as hell. "Jaxon," I breathe toward the ceiling as his mouth closes on my neck.

He suddenly takes a step back, leaving my legs dangling off the side of the counter, and sprawls his hand over his chest as it heaves. His eyes roam my body as he shakes his head and grins. With one arm around my waist, he helps me back down and turns back to the dishes.

"You better get out of here before those little whimpers make you late."

"If I didn't have a phone meeting with one of my vendors in ten minutes, I'd let you make me late. Unfortunately, I do have to go. Don't worry about the rest of those dishes. I'll finish them later."

"Absolutely not. You head into work, and I'll meet you there in a little while. Leave me your key so I can lock the dead bolt though."

Maybe the rush of blood to my nether regions has clouded my judgment, or maybe I'd like it to happen more often, but I'm about to take our relationship a step further.

"Is it too early to suggest you just put the spare on your key ring?"

He wipes his hands on a towel, then tosses it to the counter and again pulls me into his arms. But this time, there's a gentleness to his touch as he softly presses his lips against mine. My watch alarm goes off, and he lets me go, but his eyes travel down my body once more.

"I don't know how the hell to keep my hands off of you. Everytime I try, you do something so fucking sexy, I can't stand it. And that dress...that dress is something," he blurts, running his hand through his hair.

"Thank you." I pull on the dark gray fabric that crosses over my breasts, creating a deep V shape. "I just got them in the other day, and I always try to wear what I'm selling if I can. This one is a little more low-cut than I would usually wear, but I love the flowers on it. They kind of remind me of the flowers you gave me now that I look at them. I think this might become my favorite dress."

"It already is my favorite dress."

I check the time on my watch again and grab my purse. "I'm sorry, I have to go."

"Don't be sorry. Just don't be surprised when I rip that dress right off of you later."

"That's something to look forward to now, isn't it? Does that mean you're staying here again tonight?"

"I don't have to be at work until Monday. So if you want me, I'm here."

"There's no question. I want you to." I slide the strap of my wedge shoes over the back of my heel and gain about an inch of height. I'm going to be regretting these in exactly one hour, but they go so well with the dress. "See you in a little bit."

"Bye, baby."

I wasn't sure it was possible to ever be this happy in life. I thought my world was in the middle of a massive explosion about to take me down to the pits of despair. And I almost let myself get taken out by it. Then I opened my heart and let Jaxon in and I don't think anything in this entire world could ruin this happiness. Not even a curve ball to the face.

CHAPTER TEN

JAXON

IT TOOK me about five seconds after Holly walked out of her house before I threaded the key onto my key ring. Part of me still can't believe this is all actually happening. Steph texted this morning, letting me know that she's coming to Katoka Falls for the day to shop with her friend Ella. I knew it piqued her interest when I told her about all the different shops downtown, but I didn't expect her to come here. I was planning on introducing Holly to Steph over dinner sometime soon, but Holly has been so busy with the shop that I didn't want to bombard her with other things to do. Looks like Steph is going to take matters into her own hands now.

I pull up to Juneberry and knock on the glass door. Holly walks out of her office and through the shop barefoot as her perfectly plump tits bounce with each step.

"Hey," she says with a smile as she lets me in and locks the door behind me.

"Do you want me to run back to your house and get you a different pair of shoes?"

"Nah, I'll be fine."

Dusty appears as he walks out of the office, holding a white Styrofoam cup. "Hopefully I didn't put too much milk in it for you."

"I didn't see your truck outside?" I say, gritting my teeth together. I know I have to get used to the fact that Dusty is going to be around Holly all the time. But I don't have to like it.

"I'm sure it's going to be delicious. Thank you for making it for me," she says. He nods and puts the cup on the counter.

"My truck is parked in the alley behind the shop. I was just dropping a few things off but I need to run some errands this morning. I'll be back later to open." Holly nods, and he ducks back over to his shop, closing the adjoining door behind him.

"He has this new pour-over coffee maker, and since Berta...since Katoka Coffee isn't open anymore...he asked if he could make me a cup."

I put my hands on her shoulders as she glances out the window toward her favorite but now tarnished coffee shop. "That was nice of him," I say, brushing a rogue blonde tendril out of her face, and the glimmer appears again in her eyes.

"Yep." She kisses me quickly, then turns and bounces toward the back, stopping to grab the coffee on her way into the office.

"Is there anything I can do around here today?" I ask, coming around the corner to see her sliding a pair of black cat-eye glasses onto her face as she sits down at her desk. I feel as though she's actively trying to see how far she can push me before I take her back home and tie her to the bed. "Since when do you wear those?"

"They're just blue-light glasses for when I'm on my computer. Why? Do they look dorky?"

"I think between that dress, those cherry lips, and the sexy glasses, I might need to stay sitting, or everyone who comes in here is going to see how hard you make me."

She trails her finger down the center of her chest, and my mouth falls open further as she continues over her body. Holly knows *exactly* what she's doing.

I take a step closer to her, and she pushes the chair away from the desk. "You know, I think the slit in this dress is far too high. What do you think?"

She props her leg up on the desk, and the fabric spills open on either side of her. I'm forced to rearrange the bulge in my pants that's only growing from her teases. She doesn't even have to try to be sexy, but when she does, a wild hunger settles down deep, and the only thing I want is to be buried inside her.

I reach for her leg so I can run my hand down her thigh and make her feel as feral as she makes me. But just as my fingertips graze her skin, she gets out of the chair, grabs my arms, spins me around, and pushes me down.

"What are you doing?" I ask, losing every single ability to see straight.

"Shhhh." She presses those sweet lips to mine as her tits nearly fall out of the dress. I palm one of them, and she grabs my hands and places them on the armrests of her chair. "Don't move them," she instructs, her eyes burning with a mixture of fire and delight.

"Sounds like someone is trying to get a little payback," I say, grinning as she runs her hand down the center of my shirt and doesn't stop until she reaches the waistband of my pants.

"I don't know what you mean," she says, faking the

innocence in her tone as she unbuttons my pants and pulls the zipper down.

"I thought you had a call this morning," I say, swallowing hard as she continues to run her hand over the crotch of my pants.

"Already done," she whispers. Holly's gorgeous light blue eyes stare into mine with seduction and need as she slowly falls to her knees in front of me.

"Unless you want me to fuck you on this desk, you better stop now," I warn.

"Oh, I'm not stopping," she says, and I try to grab her face for a kiss, but she pushes me back. "Don't make me hold you down, baby." *Fuck.* She's using my own words against me, and I want to laugh, but I can't even fucking breathe. She tugs on my pants and I gently lift to help her wiggle my pants down just enough to free me so she can wrap her soft hands wrap around my shaft.

I lean my head against the back of the chair but never take my eyes off her. I need to consume every single detail of her face as she strokes and the rush of adrenaline flows through me. Her mouth is so close to my tip I can feel her warm breath hovering to the point of torture. She makes me insane, and I don't think this can go on much longer before I bend her over this desk and give her an orgasm incomparable to anything she's ever felt.

Her phone rings next to her computer, and she can't quite reach it with the hand that's currently not on my cock. I help her roll the chair closer to the desk, and she giggles as she silences the phone, then tosses it back.

"This feels like some forbidden office romance," I tease, and she angles her eyes up to mine, widens her jaw, and slides her warm, wet mouth over my tip.

"Oh, fuck," I growl out as I grip the armrests so hard it feels like I could snap them into pieces.

She takes me in and moans as she sucks, licks, and devours me. Holly surprises me every day, but this vixen that shows up when things get heated nearly makes me come in the first few minutes. I let out a moan as I take a fist full of hair and tug just hard enough for her to lift her eyes back to mine. I run my finger over the corner of her mouth as it stretches around me, taking me in and out. She picks up speed, her hair bouncing around her face, and my body shudders just as the adjoining door opens.

"Hey, Holly," Dusty says, and Holly tugs the chair hard, hiding under the desk but never once taking my dick from her mouth.

"She's…" I breathe hard. "She's not here."

"Oh?" Dusty questions. "Where did she go?" Holly tucked herself under the desk just enough that Dusty can't see her, but he better not come any closer.

"Uhhh…oh…" I struggle to speak as Holly takes me deep, and I hit the back of her throat. "She's at the dentist."

"Huh?" Dusty looks at his watch, confused. "Well, I forgot I had her computer mouse for the register, so I turned around." He sets it on the desk right above where Holly is. "She's going to need it when a customer comes in. I'll just wait next door until she comes back. I want to make sure it works."

"I'll—" Holly pulls me in deeply again and I swallow hard. "I'll let you know when she comes."

He smiles, looking at me weird. "Are you okay?"

"I'm good." The words fall from my mouth at warp speed because I need him to get the hell out of here. "Just go."

"Okay then." Dusty walks back to his shop and shuts the door. Holly laughs against me, and I'm almost ready to blow.

I grab her head and pull out from her mouth, standing up so hard the chair flies against the wall. With my hands under her armpits, I pull her out from under the desk and pick her up by her ass. The dress falls open, and my dick presses against the thin fabric of her underwear. She wraps her hands around my neck and kisses me hard, deep, and tasting of hot sex.

Glancing at the clock on the wall, I know we don't have much time before she's supposed to open. I take long strides to the adjoining door, flip the bolt to lock her nosey-ass neighbor out, and bring her back to the desk. She squeals as I lay her on it, tear her underwear to the side, and stop.

"Fuck, condom," I growl. "They're in the truck."

"I'm on the pill. Religiously. Please, don't stop."

It takes one plea from her, and I sink deep into her slick core. Her eyes snap shut as she puts her hand into her mouth and bites down, trying to muffle her moan. I cup her breasts as they bounce with every rough thrust, and Holly is falling apart right in front of my eyes. Her head tilts back as she arches her spine, putting her beautiful throat on display, and I satisfy the urge to wrap my hand around it and put just enough pressure to send her right over the edge.

"I warned you," I pant.

I pump into her, hoping to hear my name fall from her lips. Wanting to see her in sheer ecstasy, knowing I'm the one that caused it. She cries out as her body constricts against mine, and her thighs press into my hips, but that doesn't stop my powerful slams into her.

"Jaxon," she moans into the room as she writhes on top of the papers that are strewn on her desk. I follow right behind her, and the orgasm nearly knocks me off my feet. Through satisfied whimpers, she moves her hips as I empty inside of her.

I take deep inhales as our bodies recover from the insurmountable high. She smiles, and I lean down, hissing as doing so buries me deeper but it's never deep enough. I want her kiss and take one as every single nerve ending continues to fire shots of pleasure. The last thing I want to do right now is separate myself from her, but her phone rings again, and she quickly checks the clock.

"Whoops," she says, laughing once our breaths and the heat of the moment begins to cool. She lets out a little cry as I remove myself, and the world is cold again without her.

"You started this," I say, peppering her cheek with small kisses.

"How the hell am I supposed to just go to work now?"

"You could stay closed today, and I could take you back to your house. I'll make you lunch, dinner, and dessert in bed. No clothes, no problem."

"I want a rain check on that," she says, kissing me once more and I reluctantly remove myself from on top of her. She hops down from the desk and laughs when I smack her ass as she passes me and hobbles to the bathroom.

"You're dangerous to have around the shop," she shouts, then shuts the door.

"I'll repeat, you started it." Which gets me another heavenly laugh.

After we both clean up in the bathroom and Holly is put back together again, she heads to the front door to unlock it and take down the Closed sign. I open the adjoining door to find Dusty sitting at a small workbench in the corner with headphones on, carving a new piece.

"Hey," I shout and Dusty pulls off one side of his headphones. "Holly came…" I say, smiling and shooting him a wink. "…back."

With a confused look on his face, he nods. "Thanks."

"Anytime," I say, walking back into Holly's office.

Holly gave me a list of things I can do to help her while I'm here, and one of them includes printing off batches of online order stickers. As I print my second batch from her computer, a familiar voice echoes through the store so loudly I can hear it in the office. With all of the seducing Holly did to me this morning, I totally forgot about my sister coming here today. Stephanie has her arms around Holly as I come around the corner. She starts squealing as she grabs things left and right off shelves, hangers, and displays. One thing my sister has always had a knack for is shopping.

"Hey, Steph," I say, catching her attention, and she comes barreling toward me for a hug. Ella walks behind her with a couple of things in her hands too. I've met Ella on a few occasions, but she's a newer friend of Steph's. Ella's daughter is in the same class as Levi, and the two of them hit it off and have been hanging out together nonstop ever since.

"You have such a cool shop," Ella says to Holly. "This is totally my style. Like everything in here is right up my alley."

"That makes me so happy. Thank you."

Steph tosses her armful of treasures into my hands and continues to pick things up and pile them on. She stops at Kalina's soap display and starts smelling. "Holy shit," she says, deeply inhaling. "This smells like that strawberry pie Mom used to make."

The moment she says it, I know it hits her hard, but she just tucks the bar into the crook of her arm and moves on to the display of handmade jewelry. Before long, Steph has a pile so high we can barely fit it all onto the counter. Holly starts ringing it up, and Steph grabs all of Ella's things and piles them on top.

"Stop," Ella says in her soft voice. "What are you doing?"

"This is my treat."

"Oh, no," Ella says, removing things from the pile. "I can't let you do that."

Steph puts her hand on Ella's arm, and I notice she recoils slightly. "Listen. It's my best friend's birthday, and I'm going to buy her a gift."

"I love you, Steph, but *a* gift is not a counter full of gifts. Here, you can buy me this shirt," Ella says, grabbing the cheapest graphic T-shirt from the store and handing it to her.

"Nice try," Steph says.

I smile as my sister stands her ground, and Holly eyes me.

"Your sister is exactly like you," Holly says.

"Ew, don't say that ever again," Steph says, and we all laugh as she grabs the T-shirt from Ella and puts it back onto the pile.

"Is it your birthday today?" Holly asks Ella and gets a nod. "Happy birthday."

"Thank you."

"And that's why I'm going to spoil her." Stephanie pulls out her bank card and blocks Ella from the counter. "Because no one else does it for us, and men suck assholes."

Holly continues to giggle as I stand to the side of her, holding a bag open as she scans the items and places them in. Ella nearly chokes on her gum when Holly reads off the total, but it doesn't shock me in the least. I've been with my sister on a shopping trip to New York, where she bought a purse that was the same price as my house.

"When is your next day off?" Steph asks Holly.

"I'm closed on Mondays during the off-season."

"Good. You're coming for dinner. You have to meet Levi, and I'd love a proper sit-down meal with you."

"I can't this week, but next Monday would work."

"Perfect. Do you have any food allergies?"

"Nope. Can I bring anything?"

"How about an appetizer?"

The two of them going back and forth nearly has my head spinning. I turn to Ella, and she flashes me a meek smile.

"So how have you been adjusting to Airabelle Valley? Do you like it so far?" I ask Ella.

"It's so nice, and Saige's teacher is so welcoming and friendly. The small-town energy is so different from Chicago."

"Is that where your family is from?"

"Yeah," she says.

"How the heck did you land in Airabelle Valley from such a big city?"

"My daughter's father lives in Atlanta and I thought it was important during this age that she have both parents within driving distance. But I've had my fill of the big city life. So we got out a map of Georgia, I closed my eyes, and we moved where my finger landed."

"Geez. Good for you."

"Truth is, I've never lived in a house before. I lived in a downtown apartment. So there's a lot I need to learn about having a yard. Like how to fix a broken lawn mower for starters. Steph gave me a phone number for a Zayn's Lawncare or something like that."

I grin. "Call him. He's one of my best friends, and he'll take care of you."

"Okay," Steph says, her voice commanding the attention of the room. "We're off to find more treasures."

"More?" I ask, rolling my eyes.

"I can't believe I've never been here before. There's so

many cool places. I saw a big hand-carved Santa Claus in the window next door. That's where we're heading next."

Holly walks around the counter as Kalina walks in. "If you liked that, you're going to find a lot more to fall in love with over there. Dusty has some beautiful pieces."

"Stephanie, it's so good to see you," Kalina says, walking up and giving her a hug. "I can see you've done some damage in here."

"This place is incredible. I should have come down a long time ago when you told me to," Steph says to Kalina. "Oh, shoot, my manners. Kalina, this is Ella. Ella, this is Kalina."

The women greet each other briefly and then I walk them outside with only the few bags Steph let me carry. She's a stubborn mule when it comes to men doing things for her. Even me. Ella puts the one bag she has into Steph's trunk.

"Go ahead into the Woodshop, and I'll be right there," Steph says to Ella. She nods and heads next door. Steph turns to me and gives me a quick hug. "I'll text you when I get home. When are you heading back?"

"Tomorrow."

"You're so in love with that girl, aren't you?"

"Love is a heavy word."

"I've never, ever seen you like that. No one has ever brought a smile to your face like that woman in there just did. Love like that isn't heavy like an anvil or a freight train. It's heavy like a warm blanket that wraps you up and keeps you grounded. Don't be afraid of that kind of love, Jaxon. Because there's some of us out here so desperate to find it, we'd do just about anything."

"You'll find it too, Steph." I wrap my arm around her shoulder as she leans her head in for a second, and then she steps away. "Have fun today."

"Oh, we will," she says, losing her serious tone and jogging up to the door of Dusty's Woodshop. "Bye."

"Call me if you…"

"I'll call you if I need you," she interrupts, mocking me, then shoots me a quick smile before bolting inside.

CHAPTER ELEVEN

Holly

After a full and very busy week without seeing Jaxon, I could not be more excited to be heading to his house for dinner with his sister. We text and talk to each other every day, but it's never enough when you want to touch someone so bad. Between me being extra busy and exhausted from the first week back open at Juneberry and Jaxon having a ton of signs and car wraps to do at his work, we didn't have the time to get together. But finally, with my cucumber dill bites in tow, I'm halfway to Jaxon's house. It doesn't seem to matter to my brain that I've already met Stephanie because my nerves are through the roof. My phone rings and interrupts my eighties rock tune.

"Hello?"

"Where are you?" Jaxon's voice booms through the older speakers and makes me yelp. "What was that? Are you okay?" The panic laces each syllable as it echoes in my car.

"I'm good, honey. The volume was just too loud. I'm about halfway to your house."

"Shit," he says quietly.

"Is something wrong?"

"Yeah, Stephanie came down with the flu today. My nephew's father happens to be out of town on vacation. Which means dinner kind of got canceled."

"Oh no."

"I still want you here, of course. But I was hoping to catch you before you left so you could decide if you really want to spend the evening on the couch playing Mario Kart with a very aggressive and competitive seven-year-old."

"Are you kidding me? Why wouldn't I? But you should warn him I have many imaginary trophies from my years of experience totally dominating that game."

"She said she's going to school you in Mario," Jaxon says.

A small but mighty voice from the background gasps and says, "Yeah, right," followed by a giggle of disbelief.

"So you're about halfway?"

"Yeah, probably a little closer than that."

"Okay, be careful, please." My heart pumps a little faster in my chest every time he expresses his concern for me.

"I will. See you soon." I disconnect the call, and the music blares again, startling me. I turn it down and focus on the road. Now that I know how worried Jaxon gets when people are driving, it's easy to hear it in his voice. I wonder how many times he's said something to me in the past that seemed so trivial or a polite thing to say when he was really struggling on the inside. Jaxon has always appeared stoic and unbothered. Just goes to show that you have no idea sometimes what someone is facing inside. If he didn't tell me how bad his anxiety gets for him, I would never have known.

After driving the last stretch of highway and enjoying the peeks of evergreens amongst the bare tree limbs that will be budding soon, I pull up to Jaxon's modest house. I've been here a few times before with Kalina and River. Even though it's a beautiful home, it's not one you'd imagine someone who possesses the amount of money Jaxon does would be living in. His ranch home sits on the last road in Airabelle Valley, a few roads down from the fire department where River used to work and only a few blocks from JJ's Graphics.

The bright white trim pops against the dark gray exterior of the craftsman-style home. I park in the driveway, grab my cucumbers from the front seat, along with my purse, and head up the steps onto the L-shaped porch adorned with large lantern lights that flicker like a gas lamp. Every time I've been here, I gawk and envy how gorgeous those dang porch lights are. The large white door opens, and Jaxon steps out, taking the container of cucumber bites from me. He gives me a kiss and looks at my hands.

"Where's your bag?"

"My purse?" I look at him, confused.

"No, your overnight bag?"

Jaxon never mentioned anything about me staying the night tonight. "I just assumed I was going back home. And I have to open Juneberry in the morning, so I can't stay, even if I wanted to."

He puts on a smile, but his face tells me all I need to know. "So you're driving back home tonight?"

"I'm sorry. I have to."

He swallows so hard his Adam's apple bobs, and I know he's fighting something inside of him. But I can't help the fact that I have to go home tonight.

"All right, well. Come in." Jaxon nods for me to walk

inside, and as soon as I do, a small child runs across the room right in front of me.

"Levi," Jaxon calls, but the kid doesn't listen. He sighs and shouts, "Meatballs."

The child stops in place, slowly turns, and hops like a rabbit over to me as if he's just been controlled by a remote. I look curiously to Jaxon, who has a grin as he shrugs.

"Hi there," I say, angling my attention back to Jaxon's nephew.

"I'm Levi," he says, holding his small hand out. "It's nice to meet your acquaintance."

I shake his hand and try to hide the surprise. "The pleasure is all mine," I say, returning his proper greeting.

Then he looks at Jaxon with raised eyebrows. "This is Holly. Remember I told you she's coming for dinner tonight?"

"I remember. Can I have pretzels now?"

"You just had pretzels. Why don't we wait for dinner?"

"Can I have pretzels with dinner?"

"Sure."

Levi takes off into the other room, and I follow Jaxon into his beautiful kitchen with warm wood cabinets and white countertops. Everything in Jaxon's house is cozy, warm, and inviting. A bit of a different look than I usually go for, but for him, it fits.

"Just a fair warning, Levi can get a little out of control sometimes."

"Oh, I think he'll be just fine."

"No, not that. I mean he's…"

"Can I have pretzels now?" Levi walks into the kitchen, interrupting.

"With dinner," he says again to Levi who darts away again. "I feel bad that you went through all the trouble of making the appetizer and getting dressed up for no reason. Is there ice in this thing?"

He lifts the container of cucumber slices up to look at the bottom before setting it on the counter. I pull the top off, grabbing the dill cream cheese mixture I put into a plastic bag, and start piping it onto the cucumbers. "It's a party platter with a built-in ice compartment to keep everything cold."

"Zayn would love this."

I laugh and relish the thought of having something that Zayn doesn't. "And don't feel bad at all. These are one of my favorite things to make, but I rarely ever do for some reason. They're so easy to make."

I hand one to Jaxon after giving it the perfect swirl, and he pops the entire piece into his mouth. "Damn," he says with a full mouth. "They are really good. Levi, come here real quick."

Levi comes bouncing back into the room and up to the counter. "Would you like a cucumber?" I ask him. He wrinkles his nose and looks at me like I have two heads.

"No," he says.

"This one has a super-special sauce, but you don't have to eat one. In fact, I'm hoping you don't because I want to eat them all myself."

"You can't eat all those." Levi's voice gets higher as he holds his hand out.

I place one on his tiny palm, and he snatches it out and wipes his hand on his shirt. He looks at Jaxon like he's scared out of his mind.

"It's okay if you don't want to eat it," I say just as he takes a little bite, getting dill cream cheese all over half of his face. Jaxon tries to reach him, but I grab a paper towel and wipe his face first as Jaxon looks on as if he's in shock. I'm not sure why.

"What are you making us for dinner?" I ask Levi.

"I can't cook," he says with his mouth now full of cucumber.

"What? I thought you were making us a big turkey dinner with stuffing and mashed potatoes and green beans."

His eyes widen as he looks between Jaxon and me. "Uncle J, who told her that?" Jaxon just chuckles as he pops another cucumber into his mouth.

"That's actually a good question. What *are* we going to do for dinner?" Jaxon asks, wiping his mouth. "Since Steph was cooking tonight, I only have stuff for breakfast. You know, since I thought you would be here in the morning."

"Holly, you're coming to our sleepover too? Can we make a fort? I'm gonna make a fort." Before I can answer, Levi goes running into the living room.

"Sorry about that," he says. "I understand that you need to go home tonight so you can go to work in the morning."

"It's okay. I'll stay next time. But if you have everything for breakfast, then why don't we just do breakfast for dinner?"

"Yeah," Levi shouts from the other room as he pulls every throw blanket and pillow into a pile in the middle of the floor. "Pancakes!"

"Fairly certain you just won points with Levi. Pancakes are one of his favorites."

Jaxon starts pulling all of the ingredients out for eggs, pancakes, and sausage links. "I'll help you."

"Me too," Levi shouts, running up to us. "I wanna do the pancakes."

"Just be careful, buddy. And you need to listen real good, okay? There's hot things up here." Jaxon warms up two skillets as I put the ingredients to make the pancakes into a bowl as Levi stirs.

"Like this?" he asks, barely holding on to the wooden spoon.

"A little harder," I say.

"Like this?" Levi grabs the spoon a little harder and works it around as I pour the milk in.

"Use all those muscles you have in those arms," Jaxon says from behind us, and Levi clenches his teeth and stirs so hard it kicks up a cloud of flour. He drops the spoon into the batter and screams as he tries to wipe the flour off him.

"Maybe not that hard," Jaxon says, rushing to pick him up and taking him over to the sink.

I finish mixing everything up as Jaxon starts cracking the eggs. Levi helps me pour the pancake mixture onto the skillet as I watch closely so he doesn't burn himself. He waits impatiently, asking every few seconds if he can flip the pancakes. I take his hand and help him flip the first one, and he beams with pride.

"Uncle J, I did it," he shouts, holding the spatula above his head. He brings the spatula back down at a high rate of speed and knocks the rest of the pancake mixture onto the floor. It's everywhere. On his shirt, down his pants, the step stool he was standing on, and all over the floor.

He cries harder than the first time, and Jaxon scoops him up before I can react. "I'm sorry," Jaxon says, his eyes wandering down my pants, which are also now covered in pancake batter. "I'm going to clean him up. Leave this here, and I'll get it when I'm done. My sister has a few things in that laundry room through that door if you want to change."

Levi's little distressed face weighs on me as Jaxon carries him across the living room and disappears into the hallway. I duck into the laundry room, find a pair of tie-dye sweat shorts, and change into them. Jaxon isn't back from cleaning up Levi, so I quickly clean up and start another batch of pancakes. I set my eighth pancake onto the plate and hear small footsteps come up behind me.

"I'm sorry, Ms. Holly." Levi's eyes are red, and Jaxon stands behind him, shrugging.

"He takes things a little hard," Jaxon says.

I kneel down and look at Levi's sensitive, beautiful eyes and smile. "Those pants were too hot anyway. And it really isn't a big deal. Look," I say, stepping to the side. "All clean. Now, are you hungry because I have all these pancakes ready. Why don't you head to the table, and I'll get you some?"

His eyes light up, and he runs over to the table that sits off to the side of the kitchen.

"I never knew how good you are with kids," Jaxon says, moving to me and snaking his arm around my waist just where I like it.

"I love kids."

Something flashes in Jaxon's eyes, and I can't tell if it's fear or realization. Either way, it worries me. But this is not the time to get into that conversation again. He kisses my lips, we hear an "Ew" from Levi, and then we sit down to eat.

After a few games of Mario Kart, a round of Sorry where Levi almost peed his pants from laughing so hard when we worked together to constantly send Jaxon's game pieces back to the start, and a chocolate chip cookie, Jaxon has Levi start brushing his teeth so he can walk me out.

We step onto the porch, the cold air hits my bare legs, and I shiver. "Thank you for tonight," I say, sinking into his arms as he wraps them around me and puts his chin on my head.

"And you're *sure* you have to drive home tonight?"

"Yeah, but you can come stay with me on Friday, or if you

don't want to come to Katoka Falls, I can come back here on Sunday after I close up the shop."

"I'll definitely be there Friday."

I LAY my head against his chest, and his heart pounds almost violently. I know he's struggling. I can't imagine having to live with this much fear on a daily basis.

"I'm sorry."

"What are you sorry for?" he asks, lifting my chin.

"I know my long drive home makes you nervous."

"Holly, you could be driving to the other side of town and I would still have the same thoughts running through my head."

"Have you ever thought about getting help with that?"

"I do. Every other Wednesday." Somehow, knowing this makes me both proud of him and sad as hell. "I'm not ashamed, but I haven't really told the guys. They have their own issues, and I don't need them…"

"I won't say a word to anyone. I promise."

Jaxon slides his hand into my hair, cupping my face, and places a passionate kiss on my lips. I shiver again from the cold air, and he pulls me in close, causing our bodies to rub against each other. His lips part, and I dive my tongue inside, wishing so much that Juneberry was closed tomorrow. Rogue snowstorm, maybe? I could always just suck it up and leave early in the morning.

"Uncle J?" Levi calls from inside, and Jaxon chuckles as he breaks away from me.

"Yeah?"

Levi walks up to the open front door and looks out at us. "Can I have some pretzels?"

"You just brushed your teeth. Maybe in the morning."

"No. Pretzels aren't for the morning. I have cereal for breakfast. It's also time to read two chapters of my book. Mom says I have to."

"It is. Go get your water, and I'll be right there."

"Yay," Levi shouts and runs into the kitchen.

"I better get in there," Jaxon says, motioning inside his house.

"I'll text you as soon as I get home."

He nods, kisses me once more, then waits for me to be fully out of his driveway before closing the door to head inside. The entire way home, I can't help but think about how beautiful Jaxon and Levi's relationship is. And how amazing of a father Jaxon could be one day. But then I replay the conversation we had, and he never actually answered whether having a family is something he wants. What am I going to do if that is off the table for him?

I'm distracted by that thought as I get out of my car, walk up the steps, and my foot slides out from under me, causing me to fall hard on my ass.

"What the hell?" I ask, picking up the wooden chess piece that made me fall. I've seen a few of these in Dusty's shop, and when I hold my phone flashlight up to check, it has his symbol carved into the bottom. Why would one chess piece be on my porch? I look around, but the neighborhood is quiet. I get up, rubbing a now throbbing ass cheek, and let myself in. I stare at the chess piece, trying to figure out how the hell it got there. I'll have to ask Dusty tomorrow.

CHAPTER TWELVE

JAXON

LEVI KNOCKS repeatedly on Cole's front door until it opens. "Levi!" Cole shouts as Levi rushes him.

"Uncle Cole!" Levi pulls up his sleeve, they do their secret handshake and head inside, leaving me standing on the porch until I let myself in. This is nothing new.

Within the first few steps into his house, Cole's cat comes creeping around the corner, gives me one look, arches his back, and hisses at me.

"Freddy," Levi calls as he kneels to the ground. "Come here, boy."

Cole's evil cat hates everyone on this entire planet that dares step foot into his lair of malevolence. Except Levi. For some reason that cat has taken to him like a long-lost friend. Freddy plots my death with his beady yellow eyes as he settles into Levi's lap and gets pet.

"You want some cereal, kid?" Cole asks Levi, knowing he always wants either cereal or pretzels.

"Duh," he says, picking up Freddy and moving to the couch where Cole already has cartoons playing on the TV. And its not because he was expecting us after I called him asking about a haircut for Levi. It's Cole's regular Saturday morning routine. Only today he isn't wearing his cat pajamas.

Cole gets Levi his cereal and brings it to him on the couch as Freddy bolts across the room. Steph hates Levi eating in front of the TV but she knows what happens at the uncles' houses stays there. Especially at Cole's house. If I had to guess, Levi will always come to Cole's house for a fun, carefree time. He'll always go to Zayn when he needs help. He'll go to River when he wants to learn something, and I hope he'll come to me when he needs advice or someone to have his back. Not to mention, he's got two amazing parents that fight for him every day. He's one lucky kid to have so many people on his side. I wish Steph and I had that. Especially once our parents were gone. One thing is for sure, Levi will never be alone.

I take a seat at one of the barstools at Cole's kitchen island when the front door opens again.

"Get the hell away from me, devil kitty," Zayn shouts as Freddy goes scurrying between his feet. "Motherfucker, ass-licking, son of a…"

Cole and I laugh watching Zayn nearly trip over the small eight-pound creature as Freddy weaves in and out of his legs while he bats a mouse across the hardwood floor.

"That's not very nice, Uncle Z," Levi shouts from the couch across the open floor plan and into the kitchen.

Zayn scrunches his face, realizing what just came out of his mouth in front of our seven-year-old nephew. He moves to the couch to give Levi a high five. "I didn't know you were here, buddy."

"I know. You said a lot of bad words."

"Um...yeah, I did. Let's not tell your mom that, okay?"

Zayn knows better than anyone that Steph would have his ass if she heard him cuss like that in front of Levi.

"You should tell Freddy you're sorry," Levi says, slurping the milk from the bottom of his bowl.

Zayn sneers as Freddy prances back into the room with his favorite spider catnip toy hanging from his mouth. I swear that damn cat knows how much Zayn is afraid of spiders and gets it out every time he's here. With a snarled lip, Zayn mutters, "Sorry, Freddy," then takes the empty bowl from Levi and walks into the kitchen, where Cole and I are still laughing.

"Aren't you supposed to work today?" Zayn asks Cole while pretending to look at his watch.

"Don't you have a lawn to mow?" Cole snaps back, and Zayn rolls his eyes as he sets the bowl in the sink and grabs a sparkling water from the fridge.

"Not doing too much mowing just yet, for your information. But I was asking because I was planning on coming in for a haircut today."

"I still don't know why you trust me with a pair of clippers by your head," Cole says. "One of these days, I'm going to buzz one long line down the middle of your hair and leave it that way."

"That's cool. Ever have a yard full of grubs? I can make that happen. Birds," Zayn says, flapping his hands in the air. "Birds everywhere."

"Okay, children," I say, putting my hands up to stop them. "Levi needs a haircut, remember? That's why we're here."

As soon as I saw how long Levi's hair was when I picked

him up last night, I asked Steph if she wanted me to bring him
to Cole for a haircut. I thought I'd just bring him into his
barbershop that he owns downtown, but when I texted him, he
said we could just come to the house. Part of that is because
getting his hair cut has always been difficult for Levi. He has a
lot of sensory issues, and even though it's still hard for him,
he's gotten a little bit better with getting his hair cut. A lot of
that has to do with how good Cole is with him.

No one really knows why Cole just decided one day to
become a barber, but I think it has something to do with how
much of a dick his dad is. He was always pressuring Cole to do
something bigger and better with his life. I think becoming a
barber was his way of sticking it to his old man. But once he
got those shears in his hand, we all found out just how damn
good he is at it.

"Do I have to?" Levi groans, and he falls as dramatically as
he can off the couch and to the floor.

Zayn walks over and picks him up by the waistband of his
pants and carries him into the kitchen like a football. "Yes,
bud, you have to."

"Do you want Uncle Z to go first?" Cole asks Levi.

"Yep. But don't put that stripe down his head, or I'll be
mad at you."

"It was just a joke, kid. No worries, okay? I'd never do
that."

Cole breezes through Zayn's hair cut but it takes all three
of us to distract Levi enough to get through his. Cole is a
godsend when it comes to dealing with Levi. He stops when
Levi needs him to, will cut his hair on the floor if that's where
Levi wants to sit, and he's even cut his hair while they both
stand on the kitchen island before. We're all pretty protective

of the little guy because his first seven years of life haven't been so easy.

Especially when others misjudge and mistreat him constantly. Levi is high-functioning, and everyday tasks can be extremely difficult. The hardest part is watching strangers assume that he's a "bad kid" or just a "troublemaker". Even though I don't remotely know what it's like to be him, I can relate to a certain extent. But Steph, Isaac, and Levi's stepmom fight for him every day. I honestly believe it's the only reason he's thriving as well as he is. It's not easy raising a child like Levi. But none of us would have him any other way.

With a fresh haircut, a bowl of pretzels, and Freddy lying on his lap, Levi chills in the living room as the three of us gather around the island again.

"How did Holly coming over go with Levi?" Zayn asks as Cole leans against the counter, picking at his finger.

"Amazing. Levi even wanted to help cook. I mean, it didn't end well, but she had so much patience with him."

"Holly is like a saint, so that doesn't surprise me," Zayn says, talking to me but looking at Cole and cringing. "What the hell are you doing?" Zayn asks Cole.

"I have a hangnail, and my nail clippers broke when I used them to cut through a zip tie the other day," Cole says, still picking at his finger.

Zayn reaches into his pocket and pulls out a pair of nail clippers and tosses them to Cole. "How the hell do you do that?" Cole asks after catching them. "I need a screwdriver. Can you pop one of those out of your ass too?"

Zayn pulls a little black case from his belt, tugs on the zipper, and pulls out a multitool with a slotted screwdriver and four double-sided bits. "What size do you need?"

"That's new. I've never seen you have that before," I say and get a proud nod from Zayn.

"My mind is blown. There is nothing you don't have," Cole shouts, putting his hands on his head.

"Ask him if he has a tampon," I joke, and Cole slowly looks at me.

"Shut the fuck up," Cole says, low enough so Levi can't hear.

Zayn's chest rumbles as he laughs. "It's in the truck. Steph was with me, and it was kind of an emergency. I ran into the store, got her some, and she put a few in my glove box."

"I fucking giving up," Cole says, using the nail clippers. "You should've been a magician instead of a landscaper."

My phone rings, and I see River's name pop up on the screen. "Hey, Riv," I answer.

"We might have a problem."

It feels like I've laid in a bed of needles as a surge of urgency flows through my body.

"What kind of problem?" I ask.

"Speaker," Cole and Zayn say in unison, and I put the call on speaker.

"Holly found something odd on her porch last night."

All the fun has left the room as I look at my friends' faces, which look just as alert as I feel.

"What was it?"

"She found a chess piece. Well, according to Kalina, her foot found it. Apparently, she took a pretty good fall because of it."

The barstool goes flying behind me and makes a loud *BANG* on the ground. Levi covers his ears and jumps up from the couch. "I got him," Zayn says and rushes to Levi so I can focus on what's going on with Holly.

"Is she okay? She texted me that she got home okay last night, but she didn't say a word about that. Was it before she texted me? Did she have to go to the hospital? Maybe I should…"

Cole walks around the island and puts his hand on my shoulder. "She's fine," River says, stopping my panicked thoughts from racing out of my mouth. The rate at which my heart is pumping at the moment is too fast, and I need to focus on River's words. *She's fine. She's fine. She's fine.*

"Where did the chess piece come from?" Cole asks.

"We're not sure. Holly didn't want to make a big deal out of it, but something isn't sitting right with me. It's one of Dusty's pieces, but Holly and Kalina both went to talk to him, and he mentioned that he sold two of those sets yesterday. But he did say that they were the first two he's ever sold because those hand-carved chess sets are so expensive."

"So we need to find out who bought those chess sets," Cole says.

"Exactly. Like I said, Kalina filled me in on all of this and said that Holly thinks it's nothing."

"Out of curiosity, do you know which piece it was?"

"Yeah. The queen," River says.

"That seems…" Cole rubs his chin.

"Like I don't fucking like it," I blurt out. "I'll be there in a few hours because I have Levi until this afternoon."

Cole shouts to the living room. "Levi, want to stay with me and Freddy for a while today?"

"Yeah," Levi shouts.

"I got Levi," Cole says.

"I'll be there within an hour."

"Listen," River says. "I wanted you to know, but I'm not

sure there's anything you can do about this right now. There's no camera footage, nothing really happened—it's just weird."

"I'm on my way."

I hang up, and Cole, Zayn, and I look at each other. It's not just that Holly found some strange game piece on her porch. It's a feeling the three of us have in our guts. And I don't have to ask if they feel it. I know they do. Something is not right, and I'm going to find out what it is.

CHAPTER THIRTEEN

Holly

Kalina rushes into the office and puts her hands behind her back, swaying back and forth like she does when she's guilty of something. "What did you do?" I ask, taking my hands away from the keyboard.

"I may have told River about that chess piece and your little fall last night, and now it seems the brigade might be coming."

"Kalina," I whine, smacking my forehead.

"You know I can't keep anything from River. He called asking how the day was going, and it kind of just fell out of my mouth."

"Of course I would never expect you to keep anything from River. But you could have at least waited until I had a chance to tell Jaxon about it. We both know how these men are." The bell above the door jingles faintly. "Thank God there's a customer. I'm starting to think it's not even worth

opening the doors during the week in the off-season." Other
than opening day, the shop has been eerily quiet with only a
few customers wandering in every day.

Kalina moves into the main area of the shop but still has
her head turned into the office. "I know you don't think it's a
big deal, Holly, but with everything that's gone on around this
town the last few months, don't you feel like this is a bit
weird? Freaky, even?"

"Junebug," Arlo's voice echoes through the rafters, and
Kalina jumps as he walks up next to her. "Sorry, Kalina. Didn't
mean to scare you."

I swear my eyes almost pop right out of their sockets as
Arlo appears and sets down a bag.

"Oh my God," I cry as I launch myself out of my desk
chair and into his arms. "What are you doing here? I mean, I'm
glad you're here, but…what are you doing here?"

"Good to see you again, Arlo. I'll give you two a minute,"
Kalina says, heading into the shop.

"I just needed a visit home for a few days."

"Is Danica up front?" I ask, looking around him and into
the shop for his girlfriend.

"No," he says as he angles his eyes to the ground. "Not this
time. I know I should have called, but it was kind of a last-
minute decision. Can I stay with you?"

"Is that even a question?"

Kalina walks back into the office area and squints one eye.
"I just got a text from River and Jaxon is on his way."

"Oh no. Arlo, I need a minute to make a phone call. Just…
here." I hand Arlo my keys, holding the one that opens my
front door. "Take this one off, and you can go to the house."

I pick up my phone and call Jaxon as Arlo works to wrestle
the key off. Jaxon picks up with one ring.

"Holls, you okay? What's going on?"

"Everything is fine, honey, and you don't have to drive all the way here. My brother just surprised me with a visit, and he'll be heading to my house in a little bit. I know you heard about that stupid chess piece, but I don't think it's a big deal. The kids next door play in my yard all the time, and my best guess is it came from them. Dusty doesn't know most of the people who live here, and he said he didn't know who bought the chess sets. So it could have been the man next door for all we know."

"I'm coming anyway. You're hurt, and something feels really off."

"Jaxon, I slipped and have a little bruise. That's it. I promise you I'm completely fine. And if you drive all the way here, you're just going to sit and watch me work the rest of today. You don't have to worry about me being alone for now because my brother is here, and it seems like there might be a little trouble in paradise between him and Danica. I'd love to see you, but I'd rather do that when we can actually spend time together."

"Are you sure? I feel like I should at least come lay eyes on you."

"Think about that. You're going to drive two hours round trip just put eyes on me?"

"Yes." His serious and deep tone makes my heart swell. I don't know how someone could throw Jaxon away when all he does is care with his entire soul.

"How about we video call after I get home from work? You can put eyes on me then. Okay?"

"I wish you would've told me last night what happened."

"It was late, so I texted you right when I pulled into my driveway. I found the chess piece after that, and it was weird, but I still don't think it's a big deal. If it wasn't the kids, it could've been me, even. Dusty does have a box of random chess pieces that sits next to where he displays the carved Santas, and I had my sweater on when I brought one of my customers over there to show them Dusty's holiday pieces. I think it could have stuck to my sweater somehow."

"That seems like a far fetch."

"Either way, nothing else was off. My house was still securely locked up, and the alarm never went off." Arlo places the rest of my keys back on my desk and leans in close to listen to my conversation. "Listen, I have to go. But I promise I'll call you later."

There's silence on the line for a minute, and my heart hurts knowing the battle he's fighting. "All right. But the only reason I'm not is because my sister is still sick and wants me to keep Levi for another night. Cole said he'd keep him, but he doesn't do well bouncing all over the place. He's used to sleeping either with his parents or at my house."

"Oh, no. Tell her I hope she feels better soon. And I would feel terrible if Levi got all jumbled around just because of me. Especially when there's nothing to worry about."

"If you need me, Holls, I'm there."

"I know. I'll talk to you later, honey."

"Bye."

Arlo stands in front of my desk with raised eyebrows. "You and River's friend have gotten pretty serious since I left, huh? And what's this about a chess piece and you falling?"

"A lot of things happened while you were gone. I'll fill you in later."

"I know about poor Berta. I still can't get over that. The lights were on just now in Katoka Coffee though. Are they selling it?"

"Last I heard, her daughter is back and has plans to reopen it."

"Wren came back to Katoka Falls?" Arlo's face looks almost as broken as the day Wren left right after high school.

"Does that bother you?" I ask, raising one eyebrow from curiousity.

"No, of course not," he says, shaking his head and brushing me off. "Are you staying until nine like usual?

"I changed my hours during the off-season, so I'll be here until about seven, and then I'll be home. We can get something to eat, and then you can tell me why you're really here. Okay?"

He inhales deeply and sighs. "See you later."

I knew something was up the second my brother walked through that door. I just hope Danica didn't break his heart. Because I can't give him back everything he gave up when he decided to leave Katoka Falls.

———

JAXON'S ANGLED jawline is dimly lit by what I assume is the TV in his bedroom as he lies in bed talking to me through video. "How did the rest of your day go?" he asks.

"It was great." I nestle down into my bed and pull my cover up to my chin. "I was just anxious to get home and hear what Arlo had to say."

"Is everything all right with him?"

"I'm still not sure. Arlo said that Danica was so excited to go traveling by RV around the country. Arlo has always had that travel bug, just like our parents but was never able to do it because he opened the rock shop. I guess as soon as they got to Colorado and met up with her cousins, she changed her tune."

"How so?" he asks, turning onto his side.

The TV light illuminates his broad, muscular shoulder. I bite my lip, thinking about running my hands over his skin and remembering how amazing his mouth feels against mine. *Damn. Maybe I should have let him come tonight.*

"I guess now they're trying to talk him into opening a rock shop in Denver."

"And he doesn't want that."

"No. He's kind of pissed about it because if he wanted to own and run a rock shop, he would have kept his here in Katoka Falls. Now Danica wants to stay in Colorado, and the trip around the country is off."

"So he broke up with her?"

"Not yet, but if I had to bet, it won't be long. He does *not* want to live in Colorado, and if he opens another rock shop, he's going to do it in Katoka Falls. But if he did that, he'll have to find a place to rent to bring his shop back because Dusty is under contract, and I'm not going to screw him over just because Arlo wants to come back. That's not fair."

"As much as I'd rather have your brother next door to you than Dusty, I agree. You can't do that to the kid. And what about your brother's girlfriend? Is she going to come back to Katoka Falls too?"

"She's not having any part of that conversation. So he thought a little break might bring him a little clarity, and I think that's a great idea. But I feel bad for him. He had his dreams kind of crushed."

"That sucks. How long is he staying with you?"

"A few days as of right now. But tomorrow night, he's meeting up with Hubbard, who drove up from Atlanta to stay in his family's cabin. So he's going to stay there for a night or two."

"Is that the prick who couldn't take no for an answer?"

Disgust covers my face, and Jaxon runs his hand over his jaw. "It is. But I told you, I'm used to handling him anyway. He's been around for years and still doesn't understand that most women don't find his aggressive approach attractive."

"Why the hell is your brother friends with someone like that?"

"Because Arlo sees the good in him. I don't know how, but he does."

"I can't stand these long weeks without seeing you. Especially not after last night. How about dinner tomorrow night?" I can't stop the smile from spreading on my face, so I try to cover it up with my blanket, but Jaxon smiles just the same. "How about seven thirty?"

"Okay. But I do have to get up the next day and go into work, so you can't keep me up that late."

"Woah, what kind of man do you think I am? I never said I was going to stay the night."

"Oh, please," I say, teasing. "You and I both know you're staying the night. We'll barely get through dinner before we can't keep our hands off each other."

"Let's not talk about having our hands on each other, please. It's going to put images in my head that I won't be able to get out, and I can't just go take a cold shower to get rid of them tonight," he says, panning the camera over to Levi, who's passed out next to him. "He had a nightmare about his mom being sick and crawled into my bed."

"Oh, the poor little man," I say, placing my hand over my heart. "He's so sweet. At least it looks like he's back to sleep now though."

"Yeah, sweet. He's snoring with his foot in my back."

I laugh, and Jaxon chuckles quietly. "Well, if you need to take care of him tomorrow too, we can always reschedule."

"No we cannot. And we don't have to worry about that because Isaac will be back in town tomorrow and is picking him up after school. So I'll have plenty of time to finish my project at work and head out. Do you want me to meet you at your house or come to Juneberry?"

I laugh, and the image of Jaxon bending me over the desk comes to mind. "I like it when you visit me at work."

"I like it too. I'll see you there."

"I can't wait," I say, covering a yawn.

"Me either. But you might want to get some sleep because I need you to be good and rested when I get there."

"Good night, Jaxon."

"Night, Holls."

I hang up the video call and snuggle up in bed. The dreams I once had of Jaxon were ones of passion and desire. Although that's all still there, there's also the dream of a future because I'm undoubtedly completely in love with Jaxon Judge.

———

THERE WERE a million outfits that I could have worn today, but knowing Jaxon is coming, I chose one that is both comfortable and sexy. The only problem is my legs are sticking to the white leather on my office chair. My only options are to either take something from the shop to lay on the chair or use the olive-green suede jacket I wore over the mauve short-sleeve dress to create a barrier between the leather and what's left of my skin on the back of my legs. I guess I choose pain because I'm too damn chilly to take off my jacket and too cheap to use something from the shop. I yelp a bit every time I have to stand up.

"What are you doing over here?" Dusty asks, pushing open the adjoining door. We've just been keeping it open whenever we're both in for the day. That way, we can watch each other's shops if one of us needs to use the restroom. Having him here has been so much more than I could have asked for. I was looking for a tenant, but I got a really good friend too.

"I'm sticking to the chair."

"It's freezing outside. Why would you wear that anyway?" Dusty laughs, then disappears into his shop and comes back with a soft sweatshirt. "Here, sit on this."

My knee-high heeled boots clink on the floor as I walk to grab the sweatshirt. I put it on the seat of my chair and close my eyes as I sit down. "So much better. Thank you." The bell chimes above the front door. "And back up again," I say, giggling.

"Where's Kalina?"

"She's not feeling well today, so I told her to stay home." I pass Dusty and walk into the retail part of the shop.

A man with shaggy hair and worn clothes looks through a few items on one of my tables.

"Can I help you?" I ask kindly.

He doesn't speak but stares at me as he moves slow step by slow step in my direction. I shouldn't be afraid. This man has done nothing wrong. But I am. His eyes look desolate, lonely, maybe even empty. I blink rapidly as I try to stop my hands from shaking as he gets closer to me.

"Sir? Is there something you're looking for?" I ask again, but he doesn't stop his forward motion toward me.

"Dusty?" I yell. "Can you come here, please? Now."

It only takes Dusty a second to jog over, and once he sees

my back against the wall and this man's determination to frighten me, Dusty steps in front of me.

"Do you need something?" Dusty asks. "I have some cool things in my shop. Why don't you come with me?"

The man doesn't even acknowledge Dusty exists. "Are you okay?" I ask the man around Dusty's body but get no response.

He pulls what looks like a carved wooden bear that's missing a leg, and the leg that has broken off from his coat pocket.

"Need this fixed. Now," the man says, and I'm about to piss myself from fear. But Dusty holds his hand out.

"I can do that, but you're in the wrong shop. Come with me into my shop, okay?"

The man nods, and Dusty guides him through my office and into his shop. It's not ideal for him to go through there, but I'm pretty sure Dusty just wanted to get him away from me.

Not even a second passes before Dusty pops his head back in through the adjoining door. "Lock this door and your front door right now. This guy is…I don't know. Just lock up, and I'll tell you when he's gone."

I nod as Dusty closes the door, and I turn the dead bolt, then run to the front door and put up my closed sign as I lock that one up too. Part of me is beyond petrified. But the other part of me wonders what the man's story is and kind of feels guilty for judging him so quickly. The man obviously had something that could be fixed, and the more I think about it, the sadder I get. What if it's important to him and his heart is broken? He looks old and worn down, like he's seen the worst of the worst in life. But that doesn't eradicate how he made me feel when he was lurking toward me. I bite my nail polish straight off in the short ten minutes it takes for Dusty to text me.

. . .

DUSTY: All clear. He was just upset he broke it.

I HOP up from my desk and unlock the adjoining door, letting Dusty back in. "Thank you. Jesus, that scared the shit out of me."

"I won't lie, it did me too. But I did a quick fix with a little sanding and some glue, and he was all set. Anyway, it's safe to open back up now. I watched him get in a car and leave before I texted you. If you're okay, I have to finish an order that's being picked up tomorrow unless you want me to stick around for a few more minutes."

"No, of course not. I'm good over here now. Thanks again."

"Anytime," Dusty says, and he disappears again into his shop.

By afternoon, only a few more customers have come into Juneberry. This off-season is getting tougher and tougher. Thankfully, I have enough online orders to get me through the slower seasons, but I've filled all the orders for today, and I am too excited for my date tonight to do any real work in the shop anymore, so I've move Dusty's sweater to the chair behind the counter with the register and flip through social media. I get a little too giddy when my phone chimes.

JAXON: I'm leaving in just a little bit. Need anything?
   ME: Nope. See you soon. Be careful.
   JAXON: Always.

. . .

I SEND him a kiss emoji as the bell rings again above Juneberry's door, and the second my eyes flick up from the screen of my phone, my heart stops. The scary man is back, and this time, once the door shuts, he flips the dead bolt, locking us in.

CHAPTER FOURTEEN

JAXON

"YOU SOUND LIKE SHIT," I tell Kalina as she sniffles into the speaker, and it echoes through my truck.

"Gee, thanks," she says. "Tell Steph I'm never hugging her again."

"Hopefully, you'll be over it soon. She was feeling better when I talked to her today, so you probably only have like two days of feeling like death left."

"Noooooo," Kalina whines. "I'm over this damn sickness already. Anyway, are you heading over to Holly's?"

"I am. I want to run something by you first, but if you don't feel up to it, then don't worry about it."

"Absolu…" Kalina sneezes and groans. "Absolutely not. Tell me before I perish."

"I bought a large piece of land about halfway in between Katoka Falls and Airabelle Valley."

The gasp on the other end validates how important I think this is. "Like, today?"

"No. I bought it just before I brought the guys to your cabins for the fishing trip. I haven't told anyone about it, and it's just been sitting there. My original thought was to build a small house and create a calm, quiet place for Levi to visit. But also for me, Steph, and anyone else who wanted to use it."

"And now those plans have changed?"

"Yes and no," I say, glancing at the clock and realizing I only have a few more minutes before I reach Katoka Falls' village limits. "I still want to give that to Levi, but I think I want to move there permanently instead of making it a place to just visit or go on the weekends."

"That sounds amazing, Jaxon," Kalina says, sniffling again. "You'll be closer to Holly for sure."

"I want to be…real close."

"Yeah, I know. That's what I just said."

"I'm thinking…closer. Do you think Holly will freak out if I ask her to move in with me when the house is built? That would still be like more than six months away, but I want to ask her now so she can have some input on the design." There's silence on the line, and my heart is picking up speed with every passing nanosecond. "Kali?"

"You're serious about this," she says, sounding shocked. "Have you told her you love her yet?"

"I am very serious, and not yet. Are you thinking it's too soon?"

"I think you better establish that you love her first."

"I've been in love with Holly for months now. I hate being away from her. She calms me. Makes me a better man. You never know when your time is up. I used to be afraid of that. So afraid that I denied getting close to her. But now, my fear is never knowing what it feels like to have someone to go home to. I just don't want to waste anymore time."

"Never mind. Ask her. And make sure you say all of what you just said." Another sniffle breaks through the speakers, but this time, it doesn't sound like it's from her cold. "I'm so freaking happy for you two."

"I would've never met her if it wasn't for you. But before we get any mushier than we already are, I'm pulling up to Juneberry now. I hope you feel better."

"Thanks. Have fun tonight, and you better tell that woman how much you love her."

"I will. You have fun tonight too."

Her raspy laugh rattles my truck. "Oh, I'll be having so much fun. Bye."

I park in front of Juneberry, hop out as the excitement about all of things I want to talk to Holly about builds, and rush up to the door. Only it doesn't open. The lights are on inside, but there's no sight of Holly or anyone else. I walk next door to Dusty's Woodshop, and his door is locked too. *What the hell is going on here?* I rush to the side of the building and see Holly's car and Dusty's truck parked in their usual spots.

Pulling my phone from my pocket, I call her, but it goes straight to voicemail and a dull ache starts in my chest as my breathing gets shallow. I knock on the window, but Holly doesn't come running. No one does. The place is completely quiet, and that's when I notice the Closed sign up in the window.

Kalina would have told me if she knew Holly went somewhere with someone, but I call her back anyway.

"Again?" Kalina answers.

"Holly's car is at the shop, but it's closed up."

"What? That's weird. Although she did mention earlier about going with Arlo to get a spare key made for her house."

"But she knew I was coming. And she isn't answering her phone."

"I wouldn't put too much on that. She's always forgetting to charge it when she's at work. I usually end up plugging it in for her when I'm there."

"You think she's with Arlo? I don't know, Kalina. Something seems off," I say, knocking on the door again but a little harder this time. "What if she's like passed out in there or something? What if she fell and she's knocked unconscious?"

"I'll come with the key, and we'll check."

"Is River working?"

"Last I knew, he was out on a call. I'll just come."

"Do you feel good enough to do that? I can come pick it up from you?"

"I'll be fine, and that would just take more time. I'll be there in just a few minutes."

Even Kalina doesn't want to waste any time getting this door open, and that makes me think she's on the same page. I'd bust right through this glass if I knew she was hurt back there. But for all I know, she could be with her brother. I wish something would jump out at me to give me a sign. But Juneberry is completely silent. No movement, no usual music, nothing.

For the next five minutes, I call Holly about ten times, hoping that she'll eventually pick up. She doesn't. Kalina pulls up in her Jeep next to me, and we rush up to the front door. She puts her key in and turns the handle. I step inside first, the bell above the door ringing, and a man with a gun steps into view through the doorway to Holly's office and raises it in our direction.

"Oh God," Kalina screams as I shove her back out the door and watch her run away.

"Lock it," the man says, and I bite my cheek so hard the metallic taste coats my tongue. I lock the door and turn back to him.

"Where is she?" I ask. A smile spreads across his face, and a dark black cloud enters my soul. "If you hurt her, I'll fucking kill you."

He waltzes toward me, swinging his gun around loosely until he reaches my back and pushes the cold steel against my shirt. "Walk, lover boy."

CHAPTER FIFTEEN

Holly

Tears roll down my face from hearing Kalina scream. *Please let her be okay.* I say the words over and over in my head until the heavy boots of the man come closer. My heart aches when I hear another set of footsteps along with him. Dusty scoots further away from me, and I wonder why but don't have time to think much about it as Jaxon walks into the room with the man at his back. *No.*

Jaxon takes one look at me on the floor, my hands bound in front of me with industrial-strength tape, and his face reddens. He spins around to face the man but is met with the barrel of a gun.

"That won't end pretty for you," the man says. With the gun still on Jaxon and the lump in my throat so big I feel like I could choke, he grabs a pair of scissors from my desk and cuts Dusty's tape off his hands. "Wrap his wrists, and do it good," he says to Dusty.

Dusty hesitates, so the man moves his weapon from Jaxon to him. He closes his eyes for a moment, shoots me a look of pity, and grabs the tape. Jaxon backs away with balled fists, ready to fight. Until the gun moves to me.

"Don't," Jaxon says, his chest heaving, and sticks his arms out for Dusty. He looks at me the entire time Dusty wraps the tape around his wrists. "It's going to be okay, Holly." His voice is broken as he struggles to get his breathing under control. A bead of sweat drips down his forehead, and he winces as he's instructed to sit by the wall next to the door.

Still in his torn and dirty clothes, the tall man with a scruffy beard, dark mustache, and hair that looks like he hasn't washed it in a month smiles with bright white teeth. Dusty looks completely defeated and broken. I don't know why this man is doing this, but I'm petrified for all of us. I glance back over at Jaxon, who does not look well.

"Jaxon," I whisper, crying harder.

"You're going to be okay. Ignore me, I'll be fine," he snips out. "I'm worried." He stops to take a quick and shallow inhale. "I'm worried about you. Are you hurt? Did he hurt you?"

"No. I'm not hurt at all. Listen to me, Jaxon. You've got to breathe. In through your nose." I hiccup from crying so hard. "Out through your mouth."

Ever since Jaxon opened up to me, I've noticed him getting close to having a panic attack at least once before, so I looked up how to help someone through it.

"Focus on me and breathe."

"Aww, isn't that the sweetest?" the man asks, checking the fresh tape he put on Dusty's wrists before shoving him to the ground. He waves the gun in my direction and motions to my desk chair. "Get in the chair, *Queen*."

I fling my head in Jaxon's direction as I struggle to get up from the ground and take a seat as Jaxon shakes his head and closes his eyes. He was right about being suspicious of the damn chess piece.

"Queen?" I ask the man, and he looks amused. "Are you the one that left the chess piece on my porch?"

"I thought it was a clever warning. You don't agree?" he asks.

"What did I need a warning for?"

"Oh, it wasn't for you." He spins on the ball of his foot and looks at Dusty. "It was for him."

CHAPTER SIXTEEN

JAXON

EVERY SINGLE MOVE the man makes, I watch, analyze, and plan. It's almost impossible to stop this goddamned panic attack, but focusing on how I'm going to take him down is helping me get my breathing under control. *Control.* Such a fucked-up word for someone who always looks like they have it but never actually does.

Other than to check that I'm still where he wants me against the wall closest to the back door, most of his attention seems to be on Dusty. He's on the wall opposite me, and Holly sits in the chair in the middle of the room. Sirens start off in the distance and get louder until I can see the red and blue lights reflecting on the wall through the office door, the man grabs Holly's chair and wheels it in front of him.

"Leave her alone," I say, starting to rise from the ground.

"Sit," he says, pointing the gun at her. "I'm just warning

them not to come in here. So don't do anything stupid, or I'll just end this shit show right now."

I sit feeling helpless and watch carefully as he wheels her into the doorway, hiding behind her but showing his gun. He backs up and returns her to the middle of the room, and I finally breathe again when her frightened eyes meet mine.

"Good. Now that we have some time, Dusty," he says, tossing him a phone. "call her. Now. No more games. I'm done with this shit."

A cold chill seeps into my bones, and I shudder as I look at Dusty, hoping this man is just crazy.

"What shit? What is going on?" Holly asks.

"I see you kept your mouth shut, although a little too well. I knew you weren't pushing as hard as you should be when you didn't offer any to me earlier. Don't I look like a user to you? At least you did one thing right and kept it from the queen."

"Kept what from me?" Holly says, her eyes desperately flicking from the man to Dusty. "Why is he calling me that?"

"Shut up," the man says to her. "And you—" He turns back to Dusty and points at the phone. "—find your fucking sister. She owes me money, and I want it right now, or you'll have to carve a nice little urn for your *queen* here."

He angles the gun back to Holly, and Dusty's guilty expression makes me wish I sent him through the fucking wall the first day I met him. Deep down, I knew this fucker was trouble, no matter how hard I tried to like him. Dusty picks up the phone, dials a number, and shrugs when no one answers.

"I don't know where she is. I haven't spoken to her for a few days now."

"She's got to be here. Her boyfriend came back, so where the hell is Danica?"

I'm not sure who froze first, me or Holly. Her eyes widen as she sits up straight in the chair. "What did you just say?"

"Awww, the queen wants a story. Okay. Here's a story for you. Girl wants in on a cash cow. Man sets her up for the perfect opportunity. Only she can't close the deal. So her next option is to alter the deal and bring in her brother to take over. Except," he says, spinning again on the ball of his foot and walking slowly toward Dusty, whose head is hung. "Brother here doesn't pay up either and now mysteriously seems to have no product left. So. Where's. My. Money?"

"She took off with half of the product. I used some of the money for the deposit on the storefront."

"None of that is my problem, Dusty. It's rather sad that you just became a pawn in her game. But I knew you wouldn't give up Danica, or Katherine, or Chelle, or whatever the hell she's going by these days, unless I had something you cared about. Although I still can't believe you fell for the queen." His eyes sear into Holly as a dark, evil half-smirk comes onto his face.

"Why do you keep calling me that?" Holly asks, the frustration pouring from her mouth and it kills me inside. I will save her. I just need the right opportunity.

"Because," the man yells. "You were the most powerful piece in this game. But instead of using you to his advantage, this idiot protected you when he should have been doing his damn job. He fell for you like a horny highschooler."

My hands burn from how hard I'm squeezing my fists but I can hardly feel the rest of my body. Rage and fear shake my soul as I prepare myself to save Holly at all costs.

"It's not like that," Dusty says. "She's just a friend."

"Don't care," the man says. "Friend or lover, doesn't really matter. I saw how you protected her earlier when I came in, and it was all I needed to see."

I find it laughable that this man thought this tape would actually hold a man like me back. It's getting more difficult to wait for the right moment but I can't risk putting Holly in the line of a bullet.

"Wait," Holly says. "Are you telling me that Danica is your sister? And I don't understand, Dusty. What the hell is he talking about?"

Dusty sniffs and raises his head to finally look at Holly with tears in his eyes. "Danica planned to work in the rock shop with Arlo so she could use it to disguise the drugs. She was going to hide them in the rocks. That was the original plan. But Arlo wasn't keen on the idea of working with his new girlfriend. So she came up with a new idea and talked me into going along with her plan. She said it would only be temporary and that I could conceal it inside my wood carvings. But when we tried to rent a building down the street, we were denied and running out of time. That's when Danica came up with the idea to get Arlo to move away, knowing you'd have to find a tenant for this space. And I could move in."

"Unfuckingbelievable," I say, clenching my teeth so hard it hurts.

"You took advantage of my kindness," Holly cries. "I believed in you. You became like a brother to me. How could you?"

"I couldn't," he says, lurching forward, and Holly gasps as the man kicks him in the stomach, causing him to fall back coughing. "At first, yes. But then I got to know you, and I couldn't push it anymore like they wanted me to. For once, I found a place I felt welcomed. At least by you, anyway. So I stopped pushing it. Stopped telling people I had it. Stopped having it in the shop altogether because I was afraid to get caught. I was afraid to disappoint the one person who treated me like a human being and not a squished bug under a heavy book." Dusty lifts his hands to his eyes and rubs away the tears. "I'm sorry, Holly. I'm so fucking sorry. I didn't mean for any of this to…"

"I could have helped you get out of this," Holly says, crying. I know she cares about him and it's killing me how hurt she is right now.

My hands burn from wanting to hold her. To tell her everything is going to be okay and I'm going to get us out of here. But the man begins to pace, keeping his gun trained on one of us at all times.

"God, you're fucking useless," the man says, frustrated. "Look at you. No wonder you're a failure. Definitely nothing like that sister of yours. Then again, she is running from me like a coward. This is all your fault. You and that little tramp of a sister. It makes me sick thinking about everything I did to try to help you stay under the radar. That woman's death is on your hands too."

"What woman?" Holly says, almost jumping out of her chair.

"People with much to say only stop when they are silenced," the man says.

"He didn't do that," Holly says. "Someone was arrested for that already."

"I know," the man says, rolling his eyes. "And he's been compensated for his role."

"Oh God," Holly cries. "You're responsible for all of it. Oh my God. You killed Berta. You fucking asshole—you're going to pay for that."

"Holly," I say, trying to pull her back to the reality that he has a gun and she should refrain from tempting him.

"Danica was trying to get my brother to open a shop in

Colorado and got super pissed when he said no. She was going to use him to sell…sell…"

"You can say it," the man says with an evil grin. "Drugs. To sell drugs. You all take being good way too seriously."

"Why wouldn't she just open her own shop?"

"She can't," Dusty says. "Her credit is bad, and I'm pretty sure she's got a warrant or two in at least six states. Danica isn't even her real name."

A knock comes from the front door, and the man grabs Holly and pushes her in front of him as he walks toward the opening between the shop and the office. He forces Holly to stick her head out. "Tell me what you see?" he demands.

"There's a cop at the door."

"Only one?"

"Yes."

"How many cop cars are there?"

"I don't know. Their headlights are blinding."

I glance over at Dusty, ready to rip his esophagus straight out of his neck. Dusty mouths, "Hey," without a sound. "I'll distract him. You grab her and run out the back." The man turns to us, and Dusty acts like he's yawning, and Holly says something else to him so his attention goes back to her. "Get her out of here."

I nod, realizing that Dusty is about to put himself in a bad position to get Holly out of here.

Holly and the man walk back to the chair, and he orders her to sit, then turns back to Dusty. "Call her again. And if she doesn't answer, we're fucking done here. She'll answer to me when you're all dead."

Holly starts to sob, and I know our time to act is running out. Dusty picks up the phone and dials.

"It's not going through. The call isn't going through."

"Try again." The man waves the gun around, and every time, it makes me dizzy and cuts off the air supply in the room, but I fight through it.

"I can't get it to work. The call won't go through." I can't tell by the panic in Dusty's voice if this is part of his distraction plan, so I watch carefully, waiting for my moment.

"Give it to me, you idiot," the man says, snatching the phone from Dusty with one hand. He taps on it a few times, and his face twists in anger. "What the fuck did you do to it?"

"Nothing," Dusty says. "It's a shitty burner phone that doesn't work."

"Shit," the man says, and we finally see a bit of desperation.

"Here." Dusty rises from the ground and the man swings the gun at him. Dusty puts his hands up. "I might be able to fix it."

"Ah, that's right. She said you were good with tech stuff."

"I know a little. I just need to get this back plate off." Dusty makes faces as he struggles with the phone.

Holly looks at me with worn, exhausted eyes, and I mouth to her, "We're going to get out of here."

She closes her eyes, and her chin quivers, and another sob rocks through her body. Then she nods. She knows we have to fight to get out of this. The guy has told us too much and I don't think he was ever planning on letting us go.

"Dammit, what the hell are you doing? You're going to break it," the man yells at Dusty and snatches the phone back. He tucks the gun under his armpit, to struggle with the phone case and Dusty tackles him. I pull my hands above my head, and with the force of every single muscle in my body, I bring them down, separating them at my waist and breaking the tape as the men struggle with the gun when a shot rings out and Holly screams.

CHAPTER SEVENTEEN

HOLLY

JAXON PICKS me up and runs as my ears ring in pain as two more shots ring out. I look over Jaxon's shoulder as a whoosh of cold evening air hits my legs and see Dusty lying lifeless on the ground as the man struggles to stand.

"No! Dusty," I yell as the door shuts behind us and police begin screaming instructions on where to run to get us away from the building. I'm jostled from Jaxon's arms and put to my feet as someone searches my body for what I'm assuming are weapons, but I can hardly feel the officer's hands. Feeling numb, I look to Jaxon and see an officer telling him to slow down his breathing as he searches him. The officer pulls out a small gold metal pill box and questions Jaxon about the contents.

"They're for anxiety, and I have a copy of my prescription on my phone."

Never once would I have guessed Jaxon was on any kind

of medication. He looks at me briefly when he states what kind of pills he has, then looks to the ground. There's no way he's going to be ashamed of that. I won't let him.

"You know it's illegal to carry prescription medication in an unmarked container in the state of Georgia, right?" the officer asks.

"Charge me," Jaxon responds, wincing.

Sheriff Anderson appears at my side and touches my arm. "Oh, thank God," he says. "Thank God you're all right."

"Sir," the officer who was searching Jaxon says. "He has anxiety medication not in their proper container."

"I have a prescription." Jaxon rolls his eyes and adjusts his hands, still on the side of the police car.

"He's fine," Sheriff Anderson says, blowing off the officer. "Give them back to him, and go back to your place on the perimeter." The officer hands Jaxon his box back, and he immediately opens it and takes a pill. "Holly, what happened in there? Are there more hostages?"

"Uh…ummm…some guy and…um…" Unable to form words, Jaxon moves to me and grabs my hand. As he blurts out what went down, all I hear is "Dusty is still in there with him, but there were gunshots as we were running out. I'm not sure he made it."

"C'mon," the sheriff says to the other officers surrounding us. "Get them over to the paramedics so they can be checked out." He turns back to us and shakes his head. "We're going to get him. They're going to need some information from you and to ask some questions. Can you do that?"

"I can try," I say. "The man in there…he's responsible for Berta's murder. He said he hired someone to kill her."

"Okay," Sheriff Anderson says, patting my shoulder as I struggle to stop crying. "Just calm down. You're safe now.

We'll get all that information in a few minutes. Just take a breath, sweetheart."

"Can you let River and Holly's brother, Arlo, know we're okay?" Jaxon asks.

"Absolutely. I've instructed all of your friends to wait at the fire station with River. Last I knew, Arlo was already there. I'll make sure they know you're both safe."

"Poor Arlo," I sob into Jaxon's side as he holds me with one hand and rubs his chest with his other.

"What is it? Are you hurt?" I ask, frantically searching his body for any signs of blood as Sheriff Anderson steps closer.

"No, I'll be all right in about fifteen minutes. The anxiety," he says, lowering his voice. "It gives me chest pains."

"We aren't taking any risks. Let's go." The sheriff walks us toward a few waiting ambulances, and they try to separate us, but I refuse.

"Holly, go get checked out," Jaxon says.

"Absolutely not. I'm not leaving you."

"This isn't going to go away unless I know you're okay. Go. Let them check you out, and by the time you get back, I'll be good as new."

He cups my cheek and presses his hot lips to mine. "I love you, Holly," he says.

"I love you too," I whisper. "I love you so much." He kisses me again, and then he drops his hand, and I let the paramedic walk him to one of the ambulances as I'm led to another.

I refuse to go to the hospital because other than being completely heartbroken about what transpired inside of my beloved store, nothing is physically wrong with me. The tears haven't stopped flowing, and I just want to pretend this day never happened. The relief from being safe and free contradicts the pain and guilt I feel for the same reasons. And putting Jaxon through all of it only exacerbates the guilt.

What feels like an eternity later, I've been checked out and answered all the questions I could possibly answer. An officer gives us a ride to the fire station, and we're ambushed by River, Zayn, Cole, Arlo, Steph, and Kalina.

But it's River who gets the first hug with Jaxon. I swear I see tears in his eyes as he pulls Jaxon in and squeezes him tight. "You shoved Kalina out, man. How am I ever going to thank you for protecting her. For protecting both of them," he says, letting Jaxon go and pulling me in for a hug. "Damn. I'm sure fucking glad to see you, Holly. Jesus."

Arlo comes running from behind Zayn and Cole and pushes through them, and River lets me go so he can wrap me up. "Oh my God, Holly. Are you hurt?" he asks, stepping back and looking me over. "Fuck. Fuck. The cops asked me a load of questions about Danica. This was all my fault. I should have never listened to her. This is all my fault. Fuck."

Jaxon puts his hand on Arlo's shoulder. "She's safe." He waits until Arlo looks him in the eye, and he repeats himself. "She's safe."

"Thanks to you. I'm such a fool."

"No," I say. "She's the fool. And it's over now."

Arlo hugs me and I can feel his heartbreak.

We huddle inside the fire station and await word on what's going on inside of Juneberry. I break down in tears every few minutes, thinking about Dusty. He seemed so innocent even after I found out what he did. Jaxon refuses to leave my side and we all sit quietly around the table the guys at the firehouse usually eat at. At the request of Sheriff Anderson, an officer has been given orders to stay here with us until the scene at Juneberry is secured.

"I gave them all the information I could on Danica," Arlo says, staring at his clasped hands on the table.

"I'm so sorry, Arlo." I put my hand on top of Arlo's.

He nods. "Apparently, this isn't her first time duping a guy. I can't believe I fell for it. And it could've killed you."

"It didn't. I'm here."

The officer turns his radio up a touch and tilts his head to hear. But I don't think he meant for the entire room to go quiet at the same time.

"Scene secure. Two deceased."

Jaxon grabs me as I fall to pieces knowing Dusty is dead, and the air in the room turns heavy. Because Dusty was just a pawn in his sister's game. An outsider. All he wanted was a friend. And he had one. Me.

"I wish he would've confided in us. He didn't even want to do it. We could have helped him, right?" I cry.

"We would've," River says and Zayn and Cole nod. "But you can't control the decisions other people make, Holly. There was nothing you could do."

Steph gets up from the couch, where she's been sitting with Kalina. "Here, Holly," Steph says, handing me the box of tissues they'd been sharing.

"Oh my God. You two are sick. You should be at home resting."

"I'll go home when you go home," Kalina says.

"And you," I say to Steph. "Do you have to drive all the way back home tonight?"

"Zayn drove Cole and me."

"And I'm fine to drive. But we aren't leaving until you two are safe and at home," Zayn says.

The sheriff walks into the room and removes his hat as

everyone gets quiet to hear what he has to say. "You don't have to worry about that man anymore, Holly. He's gone."

"And Dusty too, right?" I ask, hoping everyone in the room misheard.

"I'm sorry." Unable to stop the cascade of tears, I just nod to what I already knew. "It will be quite a while before we're done with the crime scene. I think you should go home and get some rest. I'll let you know as soon as we're done and when you can reenter the building. Until then, I'll need you to stay away."

"That's not a problem," Jaxon says, speaking up for me.

The sheriff makes eye contact with everyone in the room, ending with me, and a sadness comes over them. Then he puts his tan wide-brimmed hat on and walks out with the other officer who had been with us for most of the night.

"Let's go home, Holly." Jaxon stands from the chair and tugs on my hand. When I get up, so does everyone else in the room. We walk outside, and River pulls Jaxon off to the side for a quick chat. The town is eerily quiet now as the sirens have stopped, and you can't see the reflections of red and blue flashing lights on the buildings of downtown anymore. A shiver runs through me, and Zayn immediately puts his arm around my shoulder, pulling me into his side, and rubs his hand up and down my arm to keep me warm.

"Do you want us to stay with you guys tonight?" Cole asks. "I'll sleep on your damn floor again for all I care."

For the first time all night, I let myself smile. The last time Cole slept on my floor was the night after we knew Kalina was safe.

"That's sweet of you, but you don't need to. The danger is over, and besides, I've got Jaxon and Arlo."

"I know. But you've got a group of us now. And if you need us, we're there. No explanation needed," Zayn says.

"Thanks, Zayn. I love you guys."

"We love you too, Holly," Cole says.

After hugs all around again, Arlo drives Jaxon and me back to my house. I pause on the porch, remembering the chess piece.

"Holly?" Jaxon pauses right next to me. "It's okay. Everything is over. You're safe."

He holds his hand for me and I slip mine inside his grasp as we walk inside my house.

Ten minutes later, I've stripped my clothes, and Jaxon slid my old ratty but favorite pajama dress that no one on this entire planet has ever seen other than me over my head. It's a far cry from that sexy silk nightgown I wore before but he doesn't seem to give one shit about it. Once I'm tucked safely in my bed in Jaxon's arms, I trace the valley of his pec muscles in the center of his chest and inhale deeply.

"You okay?" he asks. "Sorry, I'm going to be asking that, like, every two seconds for the next five years or until I can get the picture of that gun pointed at you out of my head."

"I'm okay. I'm just really grateful we're here right now. And that you've got me."

"I've always got you, baby. No matter what."

"Can I ask you something?"

"Always."

"Do you feel embarrassed that you need to take medication for your anxiety?"

Jaxon kisses my forehead softly. "More like disappointed in myself that I need it. My sister always called me *the big strong man* in her life. I never wanted to show her that I wasn't because she needed me to be that man for her."

"Jaxon," I say, pushing myself up on my elbow. "You will always be a hero to her. Just like you will always be a hero to me. No anxiety or medication in the world is going to change that for either of us. I love you."

"Damn, do I love hearing that come out of your mouth," he says, leaning up and pressing a kiss to my lips. "I love you too."

I snuggle back down into him and close my eyes. Being in his protective, loving arms is probably the only way I'll be able to get any sleep at all.

CHAPTER EIGHTEEN

JAXON

I COULDN'T GET work done fast enough today. Holly has been staying at my house for the last week and a half since the incident. Although I wish with every inch of my being that never happened, I couldn't love the fact that I'm going home to Holly every night more. But right after the incident happened, I put off a lot of projects that I really needed to finish. So lately, I've had to put in a lot of work at the shop to catch up. Hopefully, this is my last Sunday having to work ever because unless one of the guys messes something up that I have to fix, I should be all caught up.

River and his brother, Everest, took care of everything at Juneberry. There isn't a trace of what happened left in the place. All of Dusty's wood carvings have been removed, and the whole building has been cleaned by professionals from top to bottom. But Holly hasn't wanted to go back just yet. And I sure as hell am not pushing.

Kalina and Arlo have been running the shop, and Arlo has been staying at Holly's house while she makes herself at home here. And it only solidifies my feelings about wanting to come home from work to Holly every single night for the rest of my life. It just hasn't been the right moment to ask her about moving in together yet. But Everest has been a huge help and put me in touch with an architect who worked at lightning speed to get a blueprint of a house settled after only a few meetings. I don't know how Everest has all these connections, but I've been told it's best not to ask.

I walk through my front door to soft fifties music and a warm scent of brown sugar and chocolate hanging in the air. It takes me by surprise, and I close my eyes, breathing in the familiar smell of coming home to my mother at the end of a school day. She always baked on Fridays. Today isn't Friday, but walking in here, it feels like one. I shut the door and let the laughter of the woman I love and my favorite kid fill my whole heart. They both have aprons on, Levi's hangs all the way to his feet. Holly's eyes land on mine, she smiles at me, and the world suddenly doesn't seem so wonky anymore. For years, I've tortured myself thinking I'm just too much for people. It's this exact moment when I realize they just weren't enough for me.

"How was your day?" Holly asks, pulling another tray filled with fresh cookies out of the oven.

"It was garbage until just now." I wrap my arm around her waist, tug her to me, and kiss her.

"Ewwww," Levi squeals. "You're gross."

"What are you doing here?" I ask Levi, turning to him for a hug.

"We made cookies," Levi says, holding the plate of cookies

proudly for two seconds before he accidentally drops them all over the floor. "Oh no," he cries.

"Don't worry," I say, picking them up and sticking one in my mouth. "Five-second rule."

Levi's panic fades, and he goes back to arranging the cookies in perfect lines.

"Where is Steph?"

"Her friend Ella called while we were hanging out, and she asked if I could watch Levi for a little bit. She drove through some construction and thinks she got a nail or something in her tire."

"Oh geez," I say, pulling my cell phone out and calling my sister.

"Hey," she answers.

"Do you need any help?"

"I absolutely do not need help changing a tire. And now, thanks to me, Ella shouldn't need help to change one either."

"I didn't think so, but I just wanted to make sure you were all good."

"I'm all good, Jaxon. I'll see you in a few minutes," she says and hangs up.

"So," I say, turning back to Levi. "Did you have fun with Holly?"

"Yeah. I love Holly," he says, shoving another cookie in his mouth.

She beams at me with sweet pink cheeks and hope in her eyes. "So do I."

UNLIKE YESTERDAY, the drive to my house after work tonight isn't as chipper. I can't wait to see Holly, but I'm not looking forward to telling her about the news I got today. We've talked about the incident very little because she gets so upset. Hopefully, the therapist she found can help her deal with those emotions. The nightmares have at least started to be fewer in number. Right after it happened, she would wake up sweating with tears flowing down her face. I'd get her cooled off and calmed down, only for her to fall asleep and have the same nightmare two hours later. We're down to about one a night now. But that may change after I talk to her.

I pull into the driveway and go over what I'm going to say in my head as I stand on the porch. No matter how she reacts, I'll be here to hold her up. Who knows—maybe it will bring her a little closure, but I'll be choosing my words wisely. I push the door open and hear the same soft jazzy tunes from the fifties that she had on yesterday.

She walks around the corner with her coat and purse in hand.

"Where are you going?" I ask.

"We. We are going to meet Zayn at a little indoor plant store about a half hour south of here."

"A plant store?"

"Yeah. Joyful Leaves. It's the plant shop I bought all my indoor plants at before most of them died tragically when I moved."

"But why are we going?" Any other day, I wouldn't have even asked this question. I wouldn't care. I'd go anywhere with Holly but I need to tell her about Danica.

"Zayn said he'd help me decide on a few new plants." Her cheerful face starts to fall, and my insides begin to panic. "I need to see life growing again. Taking care of my plants made me happy. I mean...you make me happy, of course, but I just need something to take care of. Something to nurture and bring a little bit of color back."

I'd do anything that would help her get through this. "Think twenty will be enough? I can just buy the whole damn store if you want."

She laughs and falls into my arms as I hold her tight. The conversation about Danica is going to have to wait until we get back, but it has to happen tonight. Before she finds out another way.

Half an hour later, we pull up next to Zayn's truck at one of the tiniest buildings I've ever seen. It's tightly packed between two taller old buildings, only enhancing its small size.

"Are we even going to fit in there?" Zayn asks, walking around the front of his truck.

"Oh, stop it. I promise it's so cool inside," Holly says.

I know nothing about plants, and as much as I care about what Holly cares about, I don't have the brain capacity to tell the difference between a Monstera Aurea and a Monstera sport, but apparently, one is more rare than the other or something. As we walk through the three-room store, I can't tell one plant apart from the other. But Zayn and Holly are gasping at every turn, so I just follow behind and watch them in their environment. Seeing the excitement on both of their faces is worth every second spent here.

Life hasn't been easy for Zayn either. His parents are very much still around, but their relationship is strained because of what happened to him. He won't talk about it which seems to be a trend amongst us. But he won't even acknowledge his pain. And you can't even try to bring it up to him, or he'll just say goodbye and walk away. I'm not sure he'll ever get over what his ex, Nya did to him.

"Jaxon, look at how beautiful this one is," Holly says,

holding up a plant that looks just like the five hundred other ones.

"So green," I say, and they both laugh.

"Whatever you do, don't let this guy anywhere near it," Zayn says. "He killed the neon pothos I gave him."

Holly gasps. "He's right. Stay away from my plants."

I didn't think two people could spend more than thirty minutes max in a store this small. Turns out I was sadly mistaken. I could have traveled to Canada and back by the time we're at the register. Holly only puts one plant on the counter.

"You don't want anything else?" I ask her. "There were like fifteen at least that you looked super excited about. I'd like to buy you a few more."

"No," she says, looking happily satisfied with what she has. "I just need one for right now."

She opens her purse, but before she can even remove her wallet, I hand the cashier my card.

"You didn't have to," she says.

"I know I don't. But I'd do just about anything to keep that look on your face."

Zayn clears his throat and pushes three plants onto the counter. I guess he didn't have a problem buying more than one. And judging by the look of elation on his face, he got just as much out of this little trip as Holly did.

We went through a drive-thru, got some burgers, and ate them in the car on the way home. Holly found a fifties station on the radio, and I'm starting to like it myself. We didn't talk much on the ride home between eating and listening to the soothing old songs. At least they were soothing until we pulled into the driveway and my palms start to sweat.

Holly carries her plant into the house, and I make sure

everything is locked up before we settle in for the evening. I light the fireplace and lower the lights.

Holly relaxes into the corner of the couch and sighs. "I'm not going to lie, I love staying here with you. But I am eventually going to have to go back to Juneberry."

I wasn't expecting her to start this conversation. "I love you here too. But I also know you can't travel an hour back and forth to work every day."

"Are you ready to get rid of me now?" She giggles. "You vehemently agreed with me when I didn't want to go back before."

"I never want to get rid of you," I say, sitting down next to her and pulling her into my arms. She lays her head on my shoulder as I drag my fingertips up and down her skin. "I wanted to keep you safe, and since we didn't know where Danica was...I just needed you here and was relieved when you felt the same way."

She pushes off me to look me in the eye. "And now you don't need me here?"

"No, that's not what I meant." I pause for a moment, feeling Holly's concern. "They found Danica."

"Good," Holly says, crossing her arms, and a wave of anger flashes in her eyes. "Hopefully she goes to prison for a long time for what she did to Dusty and my brother."

My sweet woman's heart still feels so bad for that kid. Truth is, after knowing all the details, part of me does too. I may have had my issues with him, but he didn't deserve to go down like that. He was used and felt trapped, I get it. But it's only a small part that feels sorry for him. He was still an adult with a brain that could've made a different choice. Poor Holly though. She really felt for Dusty after he confessed that he was so grateful we'd helped him get that laser engraver machine into his shop because he lied about having friends to come help him. And the second Holly found out he had no friends, she made sure that wasn't true anymore.

"She's not going to jail, baby." Holly raises a worried eyebrow. "She's dead."

"How?" she asks, her voice broken.

"From what I understand, that guy that came looking for Danica wasn't the only one looking for her. She was found by someone else at a hotel in Atlanta. They shot the place up, killing her."

I can tell Holly is trying to stop her body from shaking, but it's out of her control. "Why was she even in Atlanta?"

Damn. I already know where her mind is going to go if I keep explaining things. "It doesn't matter. The point is, she's no longer a threat to you or to Arlo."

"Oh my God," she says, putting her hand over her heart. "Does Arlo know yet?"

"He's the one who called me this afternoon and asked me to tell you."

"Arlo must be so confused. I should call him."

Holly starts to move, but I tug on her arm, pulling her back into me. "Arlo is fine. I made sure of it when I talked to him. I think he's more angry and relieved than anything."

"Unbelievable. She was probably there scoping out another poor unexpecting man to bamboozle." Fuck, fuck, fuck. She led right into this. I try to just ignore what she said, but the curious look on her face says she knows I'm not telling her everything. "I can't believe she even came back to Georgia. What an idiot. She was looking, wasn't she? That awful bitch."

"Not exactly." Even though Arlo and I agreed that I would try to avoid unnecessary details, but I won't lie to her.

"What aren't you telling me?"

"She was already dating someone. He was at the hotel with her."

Tears fill her eyes. "That could've been Arlo," she whispers. Arlo was right. He said it would be the first thing she thought of.

"But it wasn't. Arlo is back in Katoka Falls. He's safe, and you're safe. It's over."

"That poor man," she says, sniffling. "Did they say who he was?"

I lower my head not wanting to look at her. "It was Hubbard."

"What?" she shrieks. "I have to call Arlo. I can't believe this. Why would he...why would she...what the fuck?"

I rest my hand on the side of her face, caressing her cheek with my thumb and swiping away the tears as they fall.

"Arlo is fine. I promise, he was more worried about you. But it's really over now, baby."

After another good cry, she settles down much faster than I thought she would and asks to go to bed, even though we both know it will be at least another hour or two before she's able to close her eyes.

"I don't know what I'd do if I had to face these hard nights alone," she whispers.

"You'll never have to know. I'll be here whenever you need me."

"Always?" she says, her voice trailing off.

"Forever, baby."

CHAPTER NINETEEN

Holly

It's been four weeks since I've stepped foot inside of Juneberry. In seconds, the one place that always felt like a warm hug turned into a haunted house with a real killer. But today, I'm doing it. I'm forcing the bravery I know is inside of me to come out. Because this shop is my happy place, and if I never step foot inside again, they win. And my mother didn't raise a daughter like that. Which she reminded me of when they visited.

Mom and Dad flew in shortly after what we now only refer to as "the incident." They tried talking me into going home with them for a while to Pennsylvania, but there's no way I wanted to be that far away from Jaxon. And after they met him, they understood why. Jaxon invited them and Arlo to his house, and we all had dinner with Steph and Levi. Like a family. Like old times. It was healing and comfortable and fulfilling to have everyone together. Mom liked Jaxon and

Steph but fell in love with Levi, which didn't surprise me. Dad talked for over an hour to Jaxon and Arlo about something while Steph, Mom, and I watched Levi kick my butt in Mario Kart. I was sad when they left, but they're off on another adventure.

I close and lock my front door for the first time in weeks, after staying with Jaxon. It feels good to finally have the courage to stay in my own bed last night, but not being in Jaxon's bed feels the opposite of good. Arlo is still staying at my house while he gets the rock shop back up and running and I'm glad I don't have to be alone. He's been working on it whenever he hasn't been at Juneberry. He and Kalina have been running the shop full-time, and I'm sure they're both looking forward to some time off. But first, I have to put a foot in the door.

A lump forms in my throat as I pull out of my driveway. I'm not sure what to expect. I know River and Everest took care of having the place professionally cleaned and I'm glad I didn't have to deal with that. I focus on breathing in and out of my nose as my palms sweat and my stomach twists. But as I turn the corner, a surge of emotion washes over me. And not because I'm panicking, but because I spot the crowd of people waiting by the front door of Juneberry. *My people.*

The tears are already streaming down my face as Zayn, Cole, River, Kalina, Jaxon, and Arlo wait for me. I park, throw the car door open, and jump out.

"What are you all doing here?" I ask, wiping my wet face as Jaxon jogs up and kisses me.

"You think we'd let you do this alone?" Zayn asks, holding one of the beautiful plants I passed on when we were at Joyful Leaves.

"I don't even know what to say other than thank you so much."

"Are you ready to do this?" Kalina asks, looking at me with concern in her eyes. "Honestly?"

I nod, and everyone moves behind me as I walk up to the door. I push it open, and the bell above me chimes. I thought that would be a trigger for me, but instead joy fills my heart. Jaxon squeezes my hand as I continue walking inside my shop. Once the initial shock of walking in here wears off, I realize the walls are a different color.

"It's beautiful," I shriek. "Oh my God."

"Do you like it?" Arlo asks. "We were both really nervous about changing anything in the shop because you worked so hard at decorating it. But I thought it would be a better idea to make it feel fresh and new in here. Still totally you, but different."

"I love it. I absolutely love it."

I've always gone with crisp white colors because they contrast so well with the mixture of deep greens and yellows in my plants. When I was moving my shop over here, I was less concerned about picking out wall colors than I was with just getting the place open. So I stuck with my usual bright, crisp white. But this...this is so much better. The walls are a pale salmon color, and new abstract paintings hang above our products, complementing the new shade of the room perfectly. Then my eyes land on one piece that I recognize from before. The carved wooden Juneberry picture Dusty made me. Jaxon knows the moment I lay eyes on it because he pulls me in close to his side.

"We thought you might want to keep that," Kalina says.

"Yeah, I do."

I stifle a sob and keep walking, knowing I'm about to enter

the place I was held at gunpoint. The place I saw Dusty get killed right in front of me. With my entire force of protection behind me and at my side, I step through the doorway into my office.

My breath hitches as my hand covers my mouth. "What did you guys do in here? It's gorgeous. Oh my God."

"We kept all of your old furniture if you don't like it," Arlo says, jumping in front of me. "If you hate it, just tell us and we'll change it back, okay?"

"Are you nuts?" I say, taking in the stunning warm earth tones. My white desk is gone, and there's a new desk made of rich mahogany with matching shelves that take up the entire wall. It's repositioned against the same wall as the opening to the store. The adjoining door that I used to look at when I sat at my old desk is now to my right. There are two cozy dark green chairs with cream blankets draped over them on the opposite wall that I can picture Kalina and I lounging in during our slow times. And above where Dusty lay dying on the ground is now a wall of macrame plants. "It feels so different in here. It feels like home again," I say, blinded by the tears. "Who did all of this?"

I look around the room, and every person standing here slowly raises a hand. "We're glad you like it," Kalina says. "Now, I hate to ruin this, but we have to open."

She hugs me so hard, then goes jogging to the front. River and Arlo hug me next before they both disappear into Arlo's rock shop.

Cole scoops me up in a huge embrace. "We're sticking around all day, so you'll probably be sick of us soon."

"I doubt that," I say as he moves aside to let Zayn hug me next with one arm as he holds the plant he brought in the other.

"The plant wall was all you, wasn't it?"

He nods and hands me the plant in his hand. "You've got to put this one up." He leads me over to an empty macrame hanging from the ceiling. There's something symbolic about putting it in there myself, and Zayn knows it.

"Thank you," I say, hugging him once more, and he heads over to Arlo's too.

Jaxon reaches for me, wiping my cheeks and holding my face as he presses his lips to mine.

"I'm overwhelmed. I can't believe you all did this."

"It's because we love you. All of us. But me especially and in a much different way."

I giggle as soak it all in and let their love give me the strength I need to reclaim my life back. Breathing out a loud sigh, I run my fingers over the gorgeous dark wood desk.

"You don't like the desk?" Jaxon asks.

"Oh, I do. I just think it needs a little..." I raise my eyebrow. "Love."

A low growl emits from his chest as he wickedly grins. "I can help you with that."

———

A FEW DAYS LATER, Kalina and I are working on restocking some of the items we sold out of and setting up new displays of some new spring and summer items.

"Where should we put these?" I ask Kalina as I hold up a handful of gauze fabric tank tops.

With the same smile she's had plastered on her face since I walked in this morning, she points to a round rack in our office that currently has new chunky knit sweaters on it. "If you put those together, they'll buy both while it's still cold."

"What is up with you today? You're acting weird."

"No I'm not."

The bell above the door chimes, and I stick the hangers onto the rack and walk up front.

"Welcome to Juneberry," I shout before seeing Jaxon saunter up to me. "What are you doing here?" I ask, jogging to him, falling into his open arms. and angling my head up for a kiss.

"I need to show you something."

"That sounds ominous."

"It's not. But I'm also not saying another word until we get there. So grab your purse or whatever, and let's go."

"I can't just leave, Jaxon. The store doesn't close for another four hours."

Kalina walks out and doesn't look surprised at all to see Jaxon. "I've got the store. Go."

"Ah, now I know what you're deal is today. I see you've been keeping secrets from me," I say, narrowing my eyes at Kalina as she pretends to zip her mouth shut.

"It's a surprise," Jaxon says, looking stoic and not too well.

"Are you feeling okay?" I ask, putting my hand on his chest.

He grabs it and presses a kiss to my palm. "Come on. Let's go."

Jaxon rubs his hands on his jeans at least ten times over the twenty-five-minute drive until we pull onto a bumpy gravel road.

"Where are we?"

For the first time, a sly smile crosses his face, but I can still see the anxiety in his eyes.

He parks in a large open meadow surrounded by trees and pulls a tube from under his seat.

"I'm so curious I could explode."

He nods for me to get out of the truck as he hops out, and he takes my hand the second we meet at the hood.

The crisp air fills my lungs with the scent of pinetrees and pure air. Jaxon pulls out a large white sheet of paper from the tube and spreads it out over the hood of his truck.

"Commuting an hour was out of the question. Is twenty-five minutes doable for you?"

"What?" I say, blinking at the blueprint of a gorgeous craftsman-style home.

"This is my land. I bought it a while ago and could never commit to what I wanted to do with it. I think there was a reason for that. I hadn't met you yet. This," he says, pointing to the paper, "this is going to be our house. Well, this exact house isn't set in stone. You can change it however you want to as long as you say yes to living in it with me."

This is why he was so nervous, my sweet man almost having a panic attack thinking about asking me to move in with him. But he didn't have to be so nervous. "I will absolutely move in with you, Jaxon. I love you."

"I love you too." He says, kissing me then trying to contain a smile as he continues to point at the blueprint. "White exterior, black trim, black fence, lots of room for a kid."

"Oh, Levi is going to love this place," I say, feeling the excitement soaring through me.

"I wasn't talking about Levi, but yes, he's going to love it too."

And that's when the sting hits the back of my eyes. I pull Jaxon away from the paper, get up on my tiptoes, and kiss him hard, deep, and long. An unseasonable cold wind rips through trees, making them sing. I shiver, and Jaxon has to put his phone down on the paper to stop it from blowing away.

Then he directs my attention to the trees behind us. I turn

as he snuggles up to my back and wraps his arms around me. "That's our backyard, right there. Can you picture it?" he asks.

I nod and start pointing. "Over there would be a perfect place for an outdoor kitchen. I always wanted one of those. And over there," I say, taking a step out of his grasp, "we'll have a hot tub for those cold, sexy nights."

"I like the sound of that," Jaxon says from behind me. I turn around to kiss him again, but I have to look down. Because he's on one knee, holding on to a dainty, simple gold band with a very thin line of tiny diamonds running down the center. I can't even speak or breathe or move.

"Before you, I wanted none of this. And now I can't imagine not having it with you. I want to wake up to you each morning. Breathe in your citrus skin as you lay against my chest every night. I want a white house with black trim and a yard big enough for a few kids to run in. I want to bounce my grandkids on my knee on the same porch we raise our kids on. Those are your dreams, Holly. But by loving you, they became my dreams too. And I found myself wanting those things with you more than anything else in the world. Marry me, Holly."

With shaking hands and tears of happiness streaming down my face, I nod. He slides the ring onto my finger, and my feet leave the ground as he picks me up and spins me around, peppering my face with kisses.

"I shouldn't have done this out here," he laughs, as another strong wind blows around us.

"I disagree. It's perfect." My teeth chatter as the gusts of wind keep coming. We laugh as he runs with me in his arms back to the truck. He opens the passenger-side door, places me inside and leans in. This kiss feels different. It's deep and hard but it feels like years of pent-up fear is released from Jaxon.

He gives me one more peck on the lips before letting me get a glimpse of the elegant ring on my finger.

"I know you said no diamonds, but I could *not* propose to you without diamonds. I'm sorry," he says, grinning.

"This is the most perfect ring I have ever seen in my life. I love it almost as much as I love you."

"I love you too, Holly. Forever plus a day more."

CHAPTER TWENTY

JAXON

GAME NIGHT WAS the furthest thing from our minds the last few months. Technically, I was supposed to have the next one at my house. But Cole asked to have it this time, and I wasn't about to argue.

"Are you almost done in here?" I ask Holly through a narrow crack in the bathroom door. The mirror and glass shower surround are fogged as Holly's shower steams up the room.

"Come in here," she calls, and I know that tone.

"I can't do that, and you know it. We're supposed to be there in twenty minutes."

"Jaxon, please?"

Holly squeals in delight as the bathroom door slams open. I step out of my clothes and into the shower. Water drips down her peaked nipples, and my dick is already hard.

"You realize this is about to be rough and fast, right?"

She bites the corner of her lip and stares me down like a puma daring a cheetah to a race.

"There's plenty of time later for slow and torturous. But that's not what I'm asking for."

Wrapping her hand around my dick, squeezing with just enough pressure, and stroking only increases my untamed need to make her come undone so hard she'll be walking sore for the rest of the night.

I pick her up by her ass, work her down onto my erection, and walk out of the bathroom. Dripping water everywhere, I carry her as she works herself up and down, driving me insane. I throw her onto the bed. I slide inside of her slowly as I kiss her sweetly, then thrust into her just the way she likes it. I relish in the way she screams my name as I give her all of me. There is nothing more beautiful in this entire world that watching my future wife come undone in my arms.

"WHAT TOOK YOU TWO SO LONG?" Steph asks, looking at me. "Never mind. I do *not* want to know. You two remember Ella."

"Of course," Holly says. "How was your birthday?"

The girls start talking about weddings and furniture, so I head over to Cole, Zayn, and River sitting around the table with beers in their hands.

"You want a Coke or something?" Cole asks, ready to stand from the table.

"I'll get it, anyone else need something while I'm there?"

"Hit me," Zayn says and Cole punches him in the arm. "One of these days, Cole, I'm going to knock you on your ass."

River laughs as I grab a Coke for me and a beer for Zayn.

"You've been saying that since we were twelve," River says. "But I sure as shit hope I'm around when you finally do it."

"All I'll have to do is sick Freddy on him and he'll go running," Cole says. "It's too quiet in here. Turn on the music channel, will you?" He asks River.

River grabs the remote for Cole's TV from the kitchen counter next to him and aims it across the room. He taps the remote on the table. "Why isn't this damn thing working?"

"Hand it to me," Zayn says as the women walk over and take a seat at the table. We all stare as Zayn removes three batteries from his pocket and puts them into the remote. He puts it over his head and presses the power button. "Did it work?" he asks with a happy-go-lucky smile.

"What. The. Fuck?" Cole says.

"Batteries?" River chimes in. "Batteries. You carry batteries?"

Everyone around the table stares at Zayn's ridiculous grin. "No," he says, starting to giggle. "Levi told me your remote was broken. I just assumed it was the batteries and brought some from home because I know Cole doesn't keep shit in his house."

Freddy comes tearing through the house and jumps on the table, knocking two beers over, scattering the cards, and flinging that damn toy spider right at Zayn, who screams like a girl.

"I'm going to kill that damn cat one day, Cole. I swear, I'll skin him and wear him as a hat," Zayn says, his chest still puffing.

"I'm not worried," Cole says, wiping the spills up with paper towels. "He'd kill you first, for sure."

Through everyone's laughter, I noticed Ella sitting between Holly and Steph. She's laughing too, but the way she looks at

Zayn isn't the same as anyone else in this room. And I know that look.

"Ella, didn't you need your lawn mower fixed?" I ask.

Zayn straightens his back. "What's wrong with it?" he asks, his tone no longer playful and his brows pulled tightly together on his face.

"It doesn't work. It's not a big deal right now, but once all that grass starts growing, I'm going to be in trouble."

"No you won't," Zayn says. "I can come check it out tomorrow if that works for you."

She nods, and a light pink blush takes over her pale cheeks. I flick my eyes to Holly, and without saying a word, she's thinking the same thing I am.

"I gave you his number," Steph says. "Get your phone out and send him your address."

River tries to distract everyone by shuffling the cards and announcing the rules very loudly. But everyone hears Zayn's phone ding in his pocket when Ella sends her address.

"Now, I warned you that these boys get a little rowdy," Steph says, preparing her friend. "So you're going to have to dig down deep and fight for those damn spoons if you're going to have a shot."

"I don't know what you're talking about. I'm about to kick all of your asses," she says, and the table erupts. Except Zayn, who's stuck in a position of awe.

Holly catches my eye and mouths, "I love you, but you're going down."

I mouth back, "Love you too, but in your dreams."

Zayn

I pull up to Ella's ranch house on a very big corner lot. For someone who doesn't know anything about landscaping or lawn mowers, this is going to be a lot of work. I park along the road and walk up to her open garage door with her blue sedan parked inside.

"Ella?" I call but get no response, so I walk up to the front door and knock a few times. No answer. She knew I was coming because I sent her a text like she asked me to. Even though I didn't get a response from that text.

I take a few steps before I hear the roar of a small engine coming from the backyard. The familiar smell of gasoline hits my nose, and then I hear a small scream. I take off running and find Ella struggling to control an ancient garden tiller.

I race to her side and take hold of the handles, shut it off, and set it to the side.

"Are you okay?"

"I had no idea that thing would be that strong. Holy shit." She places her hand over her heart and pops a hip.

"What are you trying to do here?" I ask, trying not to sound like too much of an asshole. I know many women who wouldn't have even tried to turn the thing on.

"I want to plant a garden. Carrots, peppers, cucumbers, you know...veggies."

"Okay, why don't you give this a rest for now, and I'll help you plot a good place for a garden, and we'll get it all prepped for you."

"I can't afford that. Plus, I kind of want the pride of doing this myself. I just have to figure out how."

"I get that. But you're planting this garden in a place that will be shaded in the morning and full powerful sun in the afternoon. It can still produce, but you run the risk of the plants overheating if you don't water them religiously."

"Okay, so maybe you could just give me a few tips and show me how to run that thing," she says, pointing at the tiller.

"I can do that. But for now, can you show me this lawnmower?"

It's impossible to keep my eyes from wandering down to her swaying hips as she leads me into the open garage. Ella is a fucking knockout. From her flawless ivory skin to her auburn hair down to her perfectly plump ass.

"It's over there," she says, pointing into the corner of the garage. As I step inside and my eyes adjust to the dim light, I die a little inside. The thing looks like it's a hundred years old.

I tug it out to the driveway just as the roar of a motorcycle engine nears and her pale face gets even paler.

"Ella? Everything okay?"

She ignores my question as she freezes, listening to the bike getting closer. "Shit," she says under her breath, and she takes off running into her house seconds before a biker stops at the end of her driveway. He stomps up to me, trying to look hard but I'm not fazed.

"Where is she?"

"She? She who?" I ask. There's no way in hell I'm giving this asshole any information.

"Ella. She's living here, isn't she?" he asks, pointing to the house and moving toward it.

"I don't know who you're talking about. This is my house. Get the fuck out of here."

"Bullshit."

He takes another step, and I calmly check the gas level in the lawn mower as I warn him to leave again. "You put one foot on my porch and you can meet my father, chief of Airabelle Valley Police. Although if I kill you first, you won't technically meet him. But don't worry," I say, standing straight and refusing to back away from his stare down. "I have lots of ways to hide your body."

"Is that a threat?"

"I don't know," I say, shrugging. "There's only one way to find out though."

"I know she's in there."

"Go ahead," I say, shooing him to the porch. "See what happens."

"So you're telling me no one named Ella Gowers lives here."

"I don't know anyone by that name."

"If you're lying to me, I'll be back."

"Okay." I shrug again. "But the same rules apply. If your foot touches that porch, consider yourself a dead man."

The man lets out a frustrated grunt, walks with an attitude back to his bike, and takes off. I wait a few minutes until I'm sure he's gone before knocking on Ella's door.

"He's gone," I say, and the door opens only wide enough for me to see Ella's patchy red eyes. "You want to tell me what the hell that was about?"

She doesn't speak, so I slowly push on the door, and she steps aside, letting me in.

"He found me," she whispers. "I can't believe he found me."

Who found Ella and why were they looking for her?
PREORDER ZAYN NOW!
Something tells me Zayn is in for a ride he could never have prepared for!

If you have read *River* and *Jaxon*, you can still get your fill on strong, protective heroes while you wait for Zayn! Check out my completed romantic suspense series, Elements of the Heart which starts with Watch Me Drown featuring Everest, River's brother!

Want to be the first to know everything?
Join C.E.'s Reading Roses reader group on Facebook!

THANK you so much for reading *Jaxon*. If you enjoyed this book, please consider leaving a review. It helps not only us authors, but also helps readers find more books to read!

Much love,
C.E. Johnson

ALSO BY C.E. JOHNSON

Elements of the Heart Series

Watch Me Drown

Watch Me Burn

Watch Me Breathe

Watch Me Land

Protecting You, Finding Us Series

River

Jaxon

Zayn

Cole

Jasper Creek

Libby Lane

Standalones

Rain

The Wrong Road Home

In the Dark Series

Done

Just One

Buried Hearts

ABOUT THE AUTHOR

C.E. Johnson wrote her first book in 2017 and hasn't stopped writing since. C.E. is best known for her romantic suspense series, The Elements of the Heart, which features protective heroes, strong heroines in danger, small town feels, and love that will have your heart swelling.

She's a dog lover, iced coffee enthusiast, and dreams of living in a cabin deep in the woods one day like so many of her characters do.

C.E. Johnson currently lives in the Midwest with her husband, two kids, and a bunch of spoiled rotten animals.

Want to know all about C.E's releases, exclusive teasers, and lots of fun?
Join C.E.'s Reading Roses reader group on Facebook!

Learn more about C.E. Johnson and her books at:
AuthorCEJohnson.com

facebook.com/authorcejohnson

tiktok.com/@authorcejohnson

instagram.com/authorcejohnson

goodreads.com/AuthorCEJohnson

bookbub.com/authors/c-e-johnson

Made in the USA
Coppell, TX
15 November 2022

86412158R00142